JOYFUL

By Shelley Shepard Gray

Sisters of the Heart series
HIDDEN
WANTED
FORGIVEN
GRACE

Seasons of Sugarcreek series
WINTER'S AWAKENING
SPRING'S RENEWAL
AUTUMN'S PROMISE
CHRISTMAS IN SUGARCREEK

Families of Honor
THE CAREGIVER
THE PROTECTOR
THE SURVIVOR
A CHRISTMAS FOR KATIE (NOVELLA)

The Secrets of Crittenden County
MISSING
THE SEARCH
FOUND
PEACE

The Days of Redemption series
DAYBREAK
RAY OF LIGHT
EVENTIDE

Return to Sugarcreek series
HOPEFUL
THANKFUL

REDEMPTION

JOYFUL

Return to Sugarcreek Series, Book Three

SHELLEY SHEPARD GRAY

AVON

INSPIRE

An Imprint of HarperCollins*Publishers*

To Mary Keane,
senior designer, HarperCollins:
Thank you for making my books come to life

P.S.™ is a trademark of HarperCollins Publishers.

JOYFUL. Copyright © 2014 by Shelley Shepard Gray. Excerpt from *Snowfall* © 2014 by Shelley Shepard Gray. All rights reserved. Printed in the United States of America. No part of this book may be used or reproduced in any manner whatsoever without written permission except in the case of brief quotations embodied in critical articles and reviews. For information address HarperCollins Publishers, 195 Broadway, New York, NY 10007.

ISBN 978-1-62953-147-2

Light shines on the godly, and joy on those whose hearts are right.

Psalm 97:11

A house is made from walls and beams . . . a home is made of love and dreams.

Amish Proverb

prologue

"Lizzie, your Randall Beiler is walking up the driveway," Elizabeth's grandmother called out from her spot next to the living room's front window. "And I say, there is certainly a sharp look in his eyes. Mark my words, that's a young man with a mission on his mind."

"Are you sure it's Randall, Mommi?" Elizabeth asked. "He didn't tell me he was coming calling today."

Her grandmother chuckled as she stepped into the doorway of the blue and white kitchen. "I may not be too spry anymore, but I certainly can recognize Randall. And I've also seen a man with his look a time or two."

"His look?"

"He looks serious and intent."

"That doesn't sound like Randall."

Her grandmother waggled her eyebrows. "Perhaps he's got something serious to ask you. I think I'll head on upstairs now. You can tell me all about his visit after he leaves."

"*Danke*, Mommi." Her grandmother really was a dear. Few other girls she knew were blessed with a grandmother who always seemed to know when to get involved—and when to give a girl some privacy.

"Of course." She pointed to Lizzie's cheek. "But you might want to brush off that flour before you greet him, dear."

"Oh!" Quickly, she swiped a clean dishcloth over her face.

Then, after wiping flour off her hands the best she could, Elizabeth quickly untied the other dish towel she'd fastened around her waist and hurried toward the front door.

Frigid air stung her cheeks as she leaned in the open doorway and watched Randall approach. Her *mommi* had been right. He was wearing a stocking cap, a thick black coat—and a very serious expression.

"I didn't know you were coming over today!" she called out. "It's a pleasant surprise."

But for some reason, her cheerful greeting didn't tease an answering smile. "You should step inside, Elizabeth," he replied with a sharp edge to his tone. "It's freezing out here and you don't have on a coat."

"It's cold, *jah*. But I'll be fine." She smiled at him. "You never used to be such a worrywart."

He took the steps, one of his boots slipping slightly on the second one. "You need to salt. Where is it?"

"In the hall closet, I think. I'll salt the steps in a minute."

"I'll do it for you now. Go get it, would you?"

"Sure." After grabbing the pail and handing it to him, she watched him carefully spread salt on her front entryway, steps, and sidewalk. As she watched him concentrate on his chore, a warm, cozy feeling floated through her. Randall truly did care for her.

What would she have done without him?

Times had been mighty tough for the past eighteen months. Her mother had fallen in love and remarried, and, after much discussion, she'd moved to Lancaster County with Milton Eicher. Since the house where Elizabeth and her grandmother lived was paid for, they'd decided to stay in Sugarcreek. Her mother had left, promising to send money to pay for their bills and basic necessities.

And at first she had. But little by little, the money came a little later each month, and never quite as much. Elizabeth had taken in sewing for extra money, but it in no way covered the difference.

But in the midst of it all had been her romance with the exceptionally handsome, exceptionally charming Randall Beiler. They'd been dating for almost two years now, and everyone was waiting with bated breath for Randall to finally ask her to be his bride. And when he did? Why, her life would be perfect.

All of her financial troubles would be over. The Beilers were the wealthiest Amish family she knew of, and Randall was head of a construction crew. She was certain that when they married, they could sell the house, her grandmother and she could move into the sprawling Beiler house, and at last Elizabeth could start counting her blessings again.

"You need to keep up with the salt or you could get hurt, Elizabeth," Randall said after he pulled off his boots and shut the door firmly behind him.

"At least I have you to keep me safe," she teased, thinking there was no harm in flirting with him a little bit. Grabbing his hand, which was still covered in a thick, black wool glove, she tugged. "Come sit down in front of the fireplace. We can light a log and I'll make you some hot chocolate."

For as long as she'd known him, hot chocolate with either whipped cream or her homemade marshmallows was his weakness. She'd always thought it was rather adorable. No one would have guessed that a man like Randall would have such a penchant for a children's drink.

"I can't have any of that. Not today." He pulled off his stocking cap, revealing his dark blond hair, hair that was usually unruly, which he battled by cutting shorter than most Amish men.

After taking a moment to yet again reflect on how handsome he was, and that he really was hers, she tipped her head. "Oh?"

"*Jah*. See, I came over here because I had something to talk to you about." He looked around. "Where's Anna Mae?"

"My grandmother is up in her room. Why?"

"I wanted some privacy."

Afraid she wouldn't be able to keep her expression neutral, she turned and led the way into the hearth room. This was it, she realized.

He looked nervous and intent. He wanted privacy, and he had just cautioned her to be more careful with the ice on the steps because he didn't want her to get hurt.

He was going to propose!

Behind her, she heard Randall sigh and shrug out of his wool coat before he sat down beside her on the couch. So very happy, she scooted a little closer to his side.

"Your cheeks are pink, Randall," she teased. Unable to help herself, she pressed her warm hands to his freshly shaved cheeks. "We need to warm you up."

He closed his eyes for a brief moment before pulling her hands away from his cheeks. "Don't."

"Why?" She scooted a little closer, so close that their legs were touching. "All I'm trying to do is warm you up. You're chilled to the bone!"

If anything, he looked even more uncomfortable, and shifted so he faced her. Then he cleared his throat. "Elizabeth, we need to talk."

"Then talk. I'm listening." Her pulse started fluttering. His brown eyes looked so serious. She never would have thought her easygoing Randall would be so nervous when he proposed.

Regardless, she knew she could hardly stop herself from smiling. Then she figured that there was no reason for her not to look happy. This was a moment she would always remember. Surely the happiest of her life.

Well, so far.

He met her shining gaze and frowned.

For the first time, she started to worry. Here she'd been thinking of her wants and needs . . . but he was a man who had a lot of responsibilities. "Randall, is something wrong?"

"I don't know."

Her mind raced. "Did something happen to one of your siblings?" Both of Randall's parents had passed on to heaven. That meant he and his siblings had to look out for one another.

"No, it's nothing like that." He cracked his knuckles. Fidgeted. "It's like this. We had a family meeting last night. Junior and Miriam are moving out. Her parents bought them a house near them."

"I'm shocked! I never thought Junior would leave until your sister Kaylene was grown."

"I was surprised, too. But you should see Junior's face. He's excited. He and Miriam are looking forward to having some privacy."

"Well, they are newlyweds. I can see him and Miriam wanting a little bit of time to themselves. After all, your *haus* is a busy place." She smiled softly, thinking that she and Randall would probably be wanting the same thing. "Wait. Are you upset about him moving out?"

"I'm happy for him. But the timing is bad."

"Bad?"

"*Jah.* Beverly has already moved to Joe's house."

Thinking of his pretty sister who had been flirting with

Joe almost as long as she and Randall had courted, Elizabeth nodded. "I know. They're living with his family, in the new wing his parents built for them. That didn't come as a surprise, though. After all, Joe farms his family's land."

"You're right. We did expect that." Rubbing a spot on the back of his neck, he sighed. "But what no one expected was for my eldest sister, Claire, to move to Charm."

She was beginning to feel like she was missing some kind of cryptic message. "Claire moved away almost two months ago."

Randall shifted. Braced his hands on his knees. "Elizabeth, what I'm trying to say is that I need to take on most of the responsibilities around the house now. Micah is older, but he's preoccupied with his schooling."

She wasn't surprised to hear him say such a thing. Micah Beiler wasn't just smart, he was close to being brilliant, or so everyone always said. He'd already earned his GED and was currently taking some correspondence courses from a nearby college.

It made sense for Randall to feel like he was now in charge of the family. "I understand," she said gently.

"That means I need to step up more."

"Uh-huh?" She still wasn't following him.

"What I'm trying to say is that we need to stop seeing each other."

She blinked. Then blinked again in confusion. "I'm sorry, but what does everyone getting married and moving away have to do with us breaking up?"

"I'm needed at home."

"But—"

"Levi is sixteen, you know. And Kay? Kaylene is a handful."

She smiled. "Randall, Kaylene is just a little girl."

"*Jah*, but she needs someone to look out for her. It's my turn to do that."

She still wasn't following. "But what about us?"

He shrugged. "I can't have everything."

But if he left she would have nothing! A lump formed in her throat. "Randall, you must see how this looks from my point of view. You've been coming over here for months now. Years."

"I know." He stood up, looking more weary than ever. "I'm just thankful that we never did something that we would regret."

"Like what?" She had dated him exclusively. She'd planned her future around him. Why, everyone had thought they'd be married by now! "Randall, we can't just quit."

"I can't do everything. I can't worry about you, too, Elizabeth. I'm sorry, but this is for the best."

"You're *sorry*?" She didn't know whether to yell or cry. Reaching out to him, she attempted to hold him any way she could. "Randall, we need to talk about this. How about I make you—"

He shrugged away her hand and ignored her offer. "Elizabeth, I need to go."

She was so angry and confused and hurt, she blurted the first hurtful thing she could think of. "You know, it would serve you right if I started seeing someone else."

He pulled on his coat. "I . . . I hope you do. You are going to make a mighty *gut frau* to some man."

She was flabbergasted. He didn't even sound jealous. Picking up his gloves, she practically threw them at him. "Don't forget these," she said as she opened up the front door for him. "And, please, watch your step," she added sarcastically. "I'd hate for you to slip and fall on your way out."

"I am sorry, Beth," he murmured, probably not even realizing that he'd used his pet name for her. "I never meant to hurt you."

"But you did." Unable to stop the tears from falling, she glared at him and hoped that one day he would feel as miserable as she did. "You have hurt me. And one day? One day I hope you get hurt, too. Then you'll know what my heart feels like."

Before she could change her mind, she slammed the door in his face.

"Lizzie?" her grandmother said from the stairs. "Is everything all right?"

Looking up into her grandmother's sweet face from her spot on the stairs, she wondered how she was going to take care of her without Randall's help.

How she was ever going to find another man who would love her and wouldn't mind taking care of her grandmother.

How she was ever going to get over loving Randall Beiler.

"*Nee*," she finally said. "I'm not all right. I'm not all right at all."

Her grandmother rushed to her side. "Lizzie, you look so sad! What happened?"

"I can't talk just yet," she blurted as the tears started to fall. "I'm sorry, Mommi, but I just can't."

Instead of pressuring her, she pulled her close with two soft arms. "Then don't talk, dear," she whispered. "All you have to do instead is have a good cry."

chapter one

Randall Beiler wasn't happy.

Perhaps that was putting things a bit harshly. Or maybe, rather, it was putting things a bit mildly.

Whatever it was, he needed something better in his life. A reason to be happy, a reason to be content. Or, as his little sister, Kaylene, was fond of saying, he needed something to be joyful about.

Unfortunately, he didn't think anything along those lines was going to happen anytime soon. Not while he had the combined weight of four of his younger siblings on his shoulders.

"Chicken again?" Levi griped as he entered the kitchen. "How many nights in a row have we had chicken? Something like eight?"

"I haven't been counting," Randall snapped. "If you know what's good for you, I wouldn't start counting, either."

"Did you grill it again?"

"Yep." Because he knew one way to cook chicken, and that was to grill it until it was almost charred.

Looking every bit of his sixteen years, Levi rolled his blue eyes. "Randall, can't you cook anything else?"

"Nope." He knew how to bake potatoes, open jars of green beans that his sister Claire had put up, and grill chicken. That was the extent of his culinary skills.

Glaring at the plate of chicken, each portion looking a bit like a hockey puck, Levi didn't even try to hide his grimace of distaste. "Couldn't you at least try?"

With effort, Randall tried not to let his temper snap. "*Nee*, Levi, I cannot. As I've said before, if you want to take over the meals, go ahead. But as long as I'm cooking supper every night, we're going to have what I can cook."

"Which just happens to be grilled chicken, baked potatoes, and canned beans," Micah said with a grin as he wandered in. "At least dinner isn't full of surprises anymore. Claire loved her mystery-meat casseroles, she did."

Randall smiled, imagining the creations their bossy sister was trying out on her newlywed husband. "I'm sure Jim is pining for a piece of blackened chicken right about now."

"Doubt it," Levi grumbled.

Privately thinking that one of their eldest sister's mystery-meat casseroles would actually be a most welcome change, Randall picked up the plate of chicken and carried it to the table. "Where are Neil and Kaylene?"

"On their way. Kaylene wanted to help Neil with the goats," Micah said as he pointed toward the barn.

"Levi, go ahead and set the table then."

"Again? I set it last night."

"And I cooked last night. Do it."

With a sullen expression, his youngest brother set the table for five. By the time he'd gotten the last of the silverware in place, Kaylene and Neil had filtered in.

Micah filled up glasses with water, then helped Randall fill the rest of the platters and carry them to the table. Then, after a brief prayer uttered gratefully in silence, they began to pass dishes and fill their plates.

Just as they'd done for all of Randall's twenty-one years. In fact, the only thing that ever seemed to change was the number of place mats they set out . . . and who did the cooking.

Just five months ago, things had been a lot different. Their three elder siblings, Junior, Beverly, and Claire, had still been living at home. Those three had been managing things for years, ever since their mother had died, soon after giving birth to Kaylene.

When their father died five years ago, they'd divided up even more duties. Beverly had taken over the house and sewing, Claire the cooking and finances. Junior had been in charge of them all, and had practically raised Kaylene by himself.

As the fifth eldest, Randall had more or less done his own thing. He'd taken a job in construction as soon as he'd gotten out of school at fourteen, and had figured he was doing his part by contributing his paycheck to the family bank account.

Junior, being Junior, had let him believe he'd been doing enough.

Now Randall realized that he'd been only doing enough for himself. He'd worked and courted Elizabeth Nolt in his spare time. He'd always planned to ask Elizabeth to marry him when he'd been promoted to a supervisor. Whenever the time was right.

But then things had happened.

Junior had fallen in love with Miriam Zehr, Joe Burkholder had finally gotten up the nerve to ask their sister Beverly to marry him, and then Claire—to everyone's surprise—had up and married Jim Weaver and moved to Charm.

Three siblings married in less than three months!

Of course, all three of them had spent many an hour discussing the pros and cons of their leaving. Junior and Miriam had even volunteered to continue living at the farm to take care of them all.

But that had rubbed Randall the wrong way. He was a grown man, not a spoiled teenager. No way was he going to ever say that he couldn't handle what his older brother had been doing without complaint for most of his life.

Therefore, he, Micah, and Neil had developed a new triumvirate. Micah did most of the farming and took his college classes. Neil continued to train dogs and breed his goats and pigs, all moneymakers.

And Randall had changed his life completely. He now worked construction only two days a week. The rest of the time he took care of the house, farmed, managed most of the finances, goaded Levi into doing his chores and get to his part-time job, and tried his best to take care of the youngest member of their family, Kaylene.

Unfortunately, it seemed that he wasn't all that good at being Kaylene's mother. And his domestic skills were sadly lacking as well.

As the meal continued in silence, Randall tried to think of something to talk about. "Kay, did you see Miriam at school today?" Miriam had helped out at the school for a bit before she and Junior had gotten married. Now she tutored when she could.

"*Jah.*"

"Why do you look so glum? I thought that would make you happy."

To his shock, Kaylene's eyes filled with tears. "Because she's . . . she's going to have a *boppli.*"

His fork clattered down on his plate. "What?"

Kaylene swiped her cheek with the side of her hand. "It's true."

"Well, that's a mighty big surprise," he murmured, feeling

a little disappointed. Why hadn't Junior told them all about the baby?

Levi turned to him in surprise. "Randall, you didn't know, either?"

"None of us knew," Micah said as he dabbed at his sister's cheek with his napkin. "Kay, how did you know?"

"Two of the kids were giggling about it. Saying Miriam looked like she was getting fat."

"I just saw her two weeks ago on Sunday," Randall said, trying to wrap his head around the story. "We all did. She didn't look fat then."

"She doesna look fat, Randall," their little sister said impatiently. "She looks like she's gonna have a baby!"

Micah stared at Kaylene through his wire-rimmed frames. "Miriam and Junior have been married some time now," he said in his patient way. "I guess it's no surprise that they are expecting a babe. Why are you crying?"

"Because now Junior is going to have his own family," she exclaimed, thick tears rolling down her cheeks. "He hardly comes over at all now. When he and Miriam have their own baby, I won't never see him no more."

"That would be won't *ever* see him *any* more," Micah murmured, absently correcting her grammar.

Kaylene scowled. "Oh, Micah, it don't matter, does it?"

"Well, um . . ." He looked at Randall for help.

Randall shrugged. They'd always depended on their smart brother to help with things like speech and grammar.

But that pause seemed to only make their sister even more perturbed.

As she looked from Randall to Neil to Micah to Levi, the tears started falling even faster. "None of you are girls!" she cried, then left the table in a rush.

Stunned, Randall watched her run out of the kitchen. Silence reigned around the table as the four of them listened to her scamper up the stairs, run down the hall, then finally slam her door.

Alarmed, Randall looked at his brothers. "What was that about?"

"I could be wrong, but I'm thinking that she nailed it on the head," Micah said slowly. "We're not women and she needs one. Bad."

"Or Junior," Levi commented. "Junior always looked after her like a mother hen."

As much as he hated to admit it, he was starting to think that Kaylene had a very good point. "She needs a girl around, doesn't she?"

"She is nine now," Levi said. "I think girls that age need women around."

Randall was pretty sure Levi was right. In the back of his mind, he seemed to remember Claire and Beverly being especially needy around that age—and when they became teenagers. "Do you think we should see if she could go live with Miriam and Junior? That might be best for her. You know she loves Miriam and she's always been closest to Junior."

Micah, being Micah, pondered that one for a long moment before shaking his head. "I don't think we should. That feels like we're pushing her on Junior, and that ain't right. They're newlyweds. Plus, if they've got a baby on the way, they've got other things to worry about."

"You're right about that, but we wouldn't be pushing Kay away. We would be trying to make her happy."

Levi frowned. "Somehow, I think that would make things worse. Besides, I don't think we're doing too bad of a job."

"We?" Randall raised his brows.

"Oh, don't act like that. You know I'm around a lot more now," Levi protested. "Plus I'm working construction with you, and I try to spend time with Kay, too. I don't think I'm doing anything worse than you did at sixteen."

"You're right." Randall sighed. Looking at his charred chicken and half-eaten baked potato, he wondered how such a bad supper had managed to get even worse. "But we've got to find someone."

"Randall, what about Elizabeth?" Neil asked after a moment's pause.

"What about her?" He didn't even care that his bitter tone had directed everyone else at the table to look his way.

"You dated her for years. Can't you get her back?"

"And why would I want to do that?"

"If you married Elizabeth, she could live here." Warming to his idea, Neil added, "Then she could cook, clean, and help with Kay."

"I don't think she's going to come running back to me just because I asked," he said dryly. "We didn't end things on a good note, you know."

"You mean when you broke up with her," Levi said.

Randall felt his cheeks heat as he remembered just how poorly he'd treated her. "Um, yeah. But listen, even if she did suddenly want to marry me, asking her to come here and cook and clean for the five of us ain't what most girls dream of doing when they get hitched."

Levi frowned. "You really don't like Elizabeth anymore? We all thought you were going to marry her."

He had, too. "All I'm saying is that some things are better in the past. Regrets are for fools, and I'm surely not that."

As his siblings slowly resumed eating, Randall felt the knot of disappointment that had settled deep inside him when he'd walked away from Elizabeth resurface.

No, he definitely didn't believe in regrets. But perhaps he was a fool after all—because he certainly did miss Elizabeth. He missed her something fierce. More than once he'd called himself ten times the fool because he'd broken things off with her instead of trying to figure out a way to make things work.

Thank goodness no one else knew how much he regretted breaking up with her.

Or how much he still loved her.

You, Elizabeth, are a fool," Elizabeth Nolt mumbled to herself. "For sure and for certain."

Leaning back on her haunches, she squinted her eyes against the morning sun and surveyed the dinky row of seedlings she'd just planted. If anything, they looked worse than the two rows of beans she'd planted yesterday.

One would think even a child could plant a decent vegetable garden; however, it seemed to be completely beyond her grasp.

"How are ya faring, Lizzy?" her grandmother called out from where she sat on the porch swing. "It looks to me like you've been taking a bit of a breather."

"I needed one, I'm afraid." After slowly getting to her feet, Elizabeth dusted off her skirts. Then, with a resigned sigh, she went to her grandmother's side. "I'm a poor gardener, Mommi, and that's a fact."

"I'm sorry to say this child, but it's true. Some days, I don't think you could get weeds to grow."

"I'm that bad?" She didn't even try to hide her amusement.

Her sweet grandmother was never one to hurt another's feelings. For her to say such a thing had to mean that she was doing a really poor job of it. "And how can you be so sure?"

"Besides the fact that we've yet to eat anything you've tried to grow . . . I could hear you coughing and sighing and grunting from here on the porch. That's never a good sign."

"Mommi, I don't grunt."

"You don't sing when you're planting, either," she quipped.

When Elizabeth sat by her side, Anna Mae grabbed her hand. "You need to face it, dear. You and gardening don't mix. We'll simply need to get our food from the grocery store like the Englischers in town."

"Mommi, you know as well as I do that we need this garden to work. Food is expensive."

"Most everything is, it seems."

That was the Lord's honest truth. Things had become very tight in the Nolt household, especially after her mother remarried and moved to Lancaster County in Pennsylvania. Though her mother had wanted Elizabeth to come along, Elizabeth hadn't been all that eager to live with a stepfather. Milton was a nice enough man, but he had particular ways of doing things, and Elizabeth knew she would have had to follow his rules.

Of course, that hadn't been the only reason she'd stayed behind. Though she'd volunteered to take care of her grandmother, everyone also knew that Elizabeth had only been biding her time until Randall Beiler finally proposed.

To her shame, she realized that she'd been hoping he would suddenly change his mind and come back to her. Realize that she could actually help him and his family once they got married.

She would have done that gladly, too. She liked looking

after other people. She liked cooking and sewing and planning and fussing.

But he never had come back. Actually, he'd never even looked back. Just as she'd never tried to convince him that things could work out. All they'd done was try to avoid each other as much as possible.

Now she was trying to take care of her grandmother on a shoestring budget and spending the rest of her time living in the silence of her regrets.

She'd lost weight and couldn't seem to lift the cloak of disappointment that surrounded her now. It was a difficult thing to realize that one conversation could remove all the joy from her life.

It was even worse to realize that she had no earthly idea how to get it back.

chapter two

"I don't know if you already know this, but you're planting your potatoes too close together," Levi Beiler said when he came to a stop just two feet away from where Elizabeth was kneeling in the dirt the following morning.

Elizabeth was so irritated she didn't even bother asking him why he had stopped by. Or what had possessed him to take an interest in her root vegetables. After glaring at the row of seedlings she'd just planted, she raised her chin to meet his gaze. "Are you sure about that?"

Levi used one finger and slowly tipped up the brim of his hat. When his blue eyes came into view, he met her gaze and nodded. "I'm real sure. Believe me, I've planted my share of 'em." With a grimace, he mumbled, "We're kind of fond of them at our *haus* these days."

"I can't believe this. Levi, I've almost finished planting the whole row."

"Um, I don't think so."

She set down her spade. "What do you mean by that?"

He stuffed his hands in his trouser pockets. "I'm just sayin' that you won't have finished much if the plants don't have room to grow. All you'll be getting is a mess of undergrown veggies. Ain't so?"

"I guess you're right. It's just so hard, though. I've been out here for three hours."

Levi looked at her crooked row, at the basket of tiny seedlings that she no doubt had paid too much money for, and sighed. With a look of distaste, he rolled up his sleeves and held out his hand. "Hand me that spade."

Hope, followed by the smallest amount of guilt, led her to pick the spade back up. "Are you sure?"

"I'm sure."

Since it was a sin to be prideful, Elizabeth handed it to him without another word. She needed help and was even willing to get it from a know-it-all sixteen-year-old.

She sat down on the hard ground and watched Levi nimbly walk to the beginning of her row. Then, without a bit of fuss, he dropped to his knees, dug up her seedlings, made each hole a little deeper, and then replanted every other one. He completed the task in under fifteen minutes.

Then, to her amazement, he started on the next row.

To say it took him less than half the time to dig each hole was putting it mildly. Actually, he looked a bit like an Englischer's fancy machine, his muscular arms making easy work of the hard soil. The entire time he didn't seem eager to speak, either. Instead, he merely continued to dig and repair.

And then, not even thirty minutes later, he handed her back the hoe and spade. "Now you'll have all the potatoes a person could want, Elizabeth." He frowned. "Probably more than you'd ever want."

"*Danke.*"

"It weren't no problem."

As she watched him brush off his hands and roll down his sleeves, she murmured, "I don't know whether to thank you again or hug you."

His head popped up. "You could do both," he said with a wry grin. She knew he was only saying such a thing as a bluff.

But because she was relieved enough to call it, she walked over, threw her arms around him, and gave Levi a little squeeze. "Thank you again, Levi. You've saved the day."

Raising his arms, he hugged her back, and then with a blush, hastily stepped backward. "Hardly that."

"I'm serious! You not only saved me hours of work, you saved me hours of frustration. I don't know how I'm ever going to be able to return your favor."

"I do."

"Oh?"

"Uh-huh. I came over to talk to ya about something, you see."

"I guess I had better listen, then. Come on in the *haus* and I'll get you something to drink. I made some lemonade this morning. I bet it's real cold by now."

"That sounds really *gut. Danke.*" At last, he smiled, showing off those dimples that were surely going to be the downfall of many a girl's heart.

As Elizabeth led the way into the house, she wondered why he'd come over. And she couldn't help but wonder about his blush when he'd hugged her.

Of course, it probably meant nothing, but the way his eyes had lit up at her offer of lemonade made her wonder if he'd come courting.

Surely he was too young for that; he was only sixteen to her twenty!

But if he was? She was going to have to let him down gently.

Her grandmother was resting so the house was dark and silent as they walked through the front room into the kitchen. At least there the room was sunny and bright. The yellow paint, blue cabinets, and white tiled countertops never failed to make her smile.

"Have a seat and I'll get you some lemonade," she said after they washed up. "I have some cherry pie, too. Made it fresh just yesterday. Would you like a slice?"

"I sure would."

She would have giggled at the speed to which he accepted the offering if not for his expression. It was one of pure bliss. Almost as if he didn't get such treats all the time.

Which was most curious. His sister-in-law, Miriam, was known to be one of the best cooks in the area.

After serving him a generous slice, complete with a dollop of whipped cream that she'd just prepared that morning, she sat down across from him.

Without a trace of embarrassment, Levi drank his lemonade like a man dying of thirst and attacked the pie like a man going into battle.

Only when his plate was scraped clean did he look up. A pained expression entered his eyes as his fork clattered onto the dish. "Sorry. I was a real pig, wasn't I?"

His obvious embarrassment amused her. "I wouldn't call you a pig. More like someone who was ravenous."

"I was, at that."

"Any special reason you're so hungry? I never have known your family to have any problem keeping food in the cupboards."

"Oh, it ain't that. It's just that no one in the *haus* can cook too *gut*."

"Oh, Levi. We both know that Miriam can cook rings around most anyone, especially any girl my age."

"She's not there. Her parents helped buy her and Junior a *haus* near them."

"Doesn't she still bring some meals around?"

"Not too often."

"What about your sisters? I'm sure they've kept you fed just fine."

"Beverly and Claire haven't come around too much, either." Looking at his plate, he said, "Junior, Beverly, and Claire seem to be more concerned with their new spouses than keeping their siblings fed."

"Hmm." She was surprised by that. Everyone in Sugarcreek knew the Beilers were an especially close family. She, for one, had always been more than a little envious of the way the eight siblings looked out for one another. Being an only child, the idea of having so much help and support sounded like a dream.

Getting up, she brought over the pitcher and refilled Levi's glass. "Where are they living? I'm pretty sure I saw Beverly and Joe walking downtown the other day."

"Beverly and Joe are living on his family's farm. Joe and his *daed* are already adding on a new wing to their *haus*."

"Ah. And Claire?"

"She and her husband moved to Charm 'cause Jim already had his own place."

"I'm sorry, I should've known all that. I guess I've been too busy with things here." Observing his expression, she realized that he wasn't staring at her like a boy with a crush. Instead, he was looking like he needed a friend.

Suddenly, Levi Beiler looked exactly like what he was—a teenager who still needed someone to mother him every now and then.

"It sounds like you all have had to make a lot of changes around your house lately," she commented. "That must be kind of hard."

"Uh-huh." He grimaced. "Now there's only me and Micah, Neil and Randall and Kaylene. We've got a lot more room, but things aren't going all that good at the moment."

"Oh?" Levi's comment surprised her. Every time she'd been at the Beiler house, it had been a bustling place. But more than that, it had been as if every member of the house worked together to make things run like clockwork. Junior, being the eldest boy, was their unofficial leader with Claire and Beverly his second and third in command. The girls had also shared the kitchen duties.

Thinking about how happy the slice of pie had made Levi, she asked curiously, "Who is doing the cooking now?"

"Randall."

With effort, she schooled her shocked expression. "I have to say I'm surprised. I didn't think he could cook well."

"He can't. Well, he can cook chicken and potatoes and heat up beans." Levi eyed his empty plate with what could only be described as a look of pure longing. "I'm really sick of canned beans."

Without another word, she brought over the pie plate, sliced another generous portion, and slid it onto his dish. Levi grabbed the carton of whipped topping, heaped another generous spoonful on top of the pie, then ate some more. "*Danke*, Elizabeth," he said around his second bite.

"Anytime." Watching him eat, she knew it was time to get to the point of his visit. "So, care to tell me why you are here? As much as I'm happy to feed you, I have a feeling you had a different reason in mind. What did you want to talk about? Did Randall ask you to come over?"

"*Nee.*" For the first time, he averted his eyes. "Randall doesn't know I'm here."

Thoroughly confused now, she made her tone a little

firmer. "Why did you come over, Levi? Please, just spit it out."

With a look of deliberation, he set his fork down. "Elizabeth, I came over to see if you'd come to work for us," he said in a rush. "Please."

Surely she had misunderstood him. "What did you say?"

"I want to hire you."

"You want to hire me?"

"*Jah*. I mean, no."

"Now I'm even more confused."

He shook his head, obviously aggravated with himself. "I mean, yes, me and my siblings want to hire you. Please."

"Because . . ."

"Because we need someone to help with all the female work around the house."

"You need a female."

He nodded. "Uh-huh. To do the cooking, especially." He wrinkled his nose. "And maybe some laundry, too. Neil's always got a bunch of it."

"You need a cook and a maid. And so the first person, the first *female* you thought about asking was me?" She wasn't sure whether she was thoroughly irritated, or maybe just thoroughly amazed at the boy's audacity.

Or maybe, more likely, she was amazed at herself. Because she wasn't dismissing his offer out of hand.

Levi winced. "It wasn't quite like that. I thought you might want to do it because you know us all."

"I see."

"Elizabeth, if you don't want to clean, you wouldn't have to. I mean, we almost have the cleaning part down good." He paused. "Well, except for the laundry. But the cooking?

Jah, we need you." He cleared his throat. "And see, Kaylene needs you, too."

"Why would you think that?"

"She was crying last night at the dinner table. Then she ran off. She misses Junior something fierce. And now that Miriam is in the, ah, family way, Kaylene is a little jealous, too. See, for pretty much her whole life my eldest brother has always taken care of her. Plus, she's nine now," he added in a rush, saying her age as if the little girl were on the cusp of womanhood. "I don't think she likes having only us men around."

The way he had lifted his chin and the way he was so obviously trying hard to look lofty and mature almost made her smile. Almost. "It's obvious you've put a lot of thought into this."

Levi stood up and carried his plate to the sink, his manner far more relaxed now that the cat was out of the bag. "Uh-huh. See, I was talking about everything with Micah early this morning and he suggested that I come out and ask if you'd consider working for us."

"Are you sure that Randall didn't put you up to it?"

"Oh, *nee*. He'd get mad if he knew I came over here."

"Is that right?"

"Uh-huh. On account that he used to court you and all," he explained as he returned to the table and stood behind his chair.

The "used to" reminder stung. But warring with her impulse to refuse Levi outright was the idea of bringing in some much-needed money.

And the sight of that half-eaten cherry pie. There had been something so heart-wrenching about watching a hungry teenager gobble it up. A teenager who hadn't had a mother in almost nine years.

If she didn't help them out, who would?

"Levi, I don't know if I can get away from my responsibilities here," she said as gently as she could. "I take care of my *mommi*, you know. She needs me."

He winced. "I forgot about your grandmother." After stewing on that for a second, he brightened. "But maybe you could just help us out a couple of days a week?" he asked after a pause. "Even if you only came over for a couple of hours at a time, it would be real helpful. If, you know, you wouldn't mind."

"Ah." Her heart went out to him, it surely did. But what he was asking would open up a barrel of trouble. She would have to cook for four men, one of whom was Randall. And, of course, she'd have to be away from her grandmother.

But she knew the real reason for her hesitation was Randall. What would she do if she had to be around Randall all the time?

"Don't forget that we'd pay you," Levi added in a rush. "Micah told me to make sure I mentioned that."

That caught her off guard. "I see. I wonder why."

Levi averted his eyes. "Don't be mad, but some folks have been talking about you."

"Oh?"

"Uh-huh. A couple of people thought you might be having some money problems."

Now she was sure she was blushing with him. "People are talking about me?" They knew she was struggling? That was horrifying!

"I, personally, haven't heard too much. But Micah has. And, well, you know . . . people like to share news."

She took pity on him and said what they were both thinking. "Everyone knows that my mother remarried and moved on."

"Randall did court you for two years, Elizabeth. Micah and I weren't gossiping about you. It's just that, well, we got to know you real well. Micah said he remembered that sometimes you were anxious about paying your taxes and such."

The awkward reminder hit her hard. She supposed it did make sense that everyone in the Beiler family would be aware of her financial situation. She'd certainly shared a lot of her worries with Randall . . . back when she thought they were mere months away from marriage.

As the silence between them grew, Levi grabbed his hat and slapped it on his head. "I'm sorry if I said something I shouldn't of."

"No, it's okay. I mean, you were only speaking your mind."

"Um, Elizabeth, please say you'll think about cooking and cleaning for us. We really need your help."

Determined to lessen the awkwardness, she pointed to the pie plate. "And maybe bake you a pie or two?"

"I'd love more pie." Levi grinned. "And maybe something besides potatoes, too. If I never eat another baked potato it will be too soon." Just as he entered the hallway, he turned. "So what do you say?"

There were a lot of things she could say. Things she should say. The top of the list was that she was going to need time to think things through.

But there was something about the yearning in Levi's eyes that melted her heart. After all, she knew what it was like to be helpless to make things different.

Before she knew it, she nodded. "I'll come by tomorrow and cook supper. But we don't need to talk about how much to pay me yet. I'll come over tomorrow, as a friend and neighbor."

Levi frowned. "Micah was pretty sure we needed to pay ya . . ."

"I'll talk to him about that when I see him. How about that?"

Pure relief entered his expression. "That sounds real *gut*. *Danke*, Elizabeth."

And with that, he tore out of the house, taking with him almost half a pie in his stomach.

And leaving her wondering what in the world she'd just agreed to and, more important, why. Had she just agreed to cook supper because she felt sorry for Kaylene and was amused by Levi?

Or did it have more to do with the fact that she was going to get an opportunity to be around Randall again? And that she was slowly beginning to realize that she might have misjudged him?

The moment that thought popped into her head, she firmly pushed it aside. The last thing in the world she needed was to start having doubts about her feelings for Randall. She needed him out of her system, not back in her heart.

"I only agreed to this because Levi Beiler is such a charmer," she said out loud.

Maybe if she kept saying it, she might even believe it, too.

chapter three

Judith Knox almost felt like a "real" mother. Almost.

As she sat at the long, scarred table in her parents' home, little James propped on her lap, she knew that she'd surely never felt happier.

Fostering a sweet baby like James had been one of the best experiences of her life. The only negative thing—as far as she could tell—was that there was always a sense that James could be taken from her at any time. And while Ben constantly reminded her of the definition of "fostering," saying that the social worker had only entrusted James to be in their care for a short time, she was still having trouble coming to grips with it.

Already, she loved the baby so much, she couldn't imagine her life without him.

"Judith, I think little James has almost doubled in size!" her sister-in-law Rebecca, Caleb's wife, declared. "He sure seems to be a happy baby."

"He is. He sleeps *gut*, too," Judith answered. Turning to her husband, she said, "Right, Ben?"

"He does, except when he's teething. Which he seems to be constantly doing."

"That's a little early. I mean he's only four months old, isn't he?" Rebecca asked.

"That is correct," Judith said proudly. "We've now had

him for a little over three months." Unable to help herself, she gave James another little hug and kissed the top of his head for good measure. "Sometimes I can hardly remember what our life was like before we got him."

"But you're gonna have to give him back soon, right?" Anson asked.

Her pesky brother's voice cut through the haze of happiness like a dull knife. "Anson, I can't believe you just said that."

Anson looked at their parents. "What did I say wrong? I thought James was only yours for a little while, on account that he's a foster baby. He's going to go back to his real *mamm* one day soon, right?"

The whole table—all ten people—retreated into silence. If Judith hadn't been holding James and felt the reassuring touch of her husband's hand between her shoulder blades, she feared she would have burst into tears. Or, more likely, yelled at her little brother.

All his life, Anson had had a knack for continually saying exactly what was on his mind. He had no filter; if he thought it, he blurted it. Anytime, anyplace. Unfortunately, he almost always managed to hurt someone's feelings.

Slowly, she took a deep breath and tried to remember that her little brother wasn't trying to be hurtful. No good would come from making a big fuss.

"It's not all just a matter of giving him back," Ben explained in a matter-of-fact tone. "Kendra is still in jail and isn't supposed to be out for another year or so. And until she is ready to take care of him full-time, we've been entrusted to be James's temporary parents. It's a *wonderful-gut* blessing." He cleared his throat. "Right, Judith?"

"Oh, *jah*." And it was true. They absolutely knew that James wasn't going to be their baby to raise. But that hadn't stopped her, in her weakest moments, from pretending that he would be.

Gradually, conversation began again, at first stilted, but then flowing easily as Caleb began telling stories about life at the brick factory where he worked.

Two hours later, after helping to clean up the dishes and the short buggy ride back to their house in town, Judith stood by Ben's side as they tucked James in.

Later, she sat in the rocking chair by the crib and watched him sleep. Praying for his comfort and, selfishly, for her to somehow gather the courage to find the strength to be able to give James back to his mother one day.

It shamed her that she would ever even consider not wanting him to go back to his mother. But that was why she was human, she realized. She was flawed and imperfect. And where James was concerned, more than a little selfish. She needed the Lord's guiding hand—and His grace—as much as anyone she knew. It was going to take a lot of prayer to smile when it was time to place James in his mother's arms and then turn and walk away.

As she continued to rock, she heard Ben go downstairs. Noises drifted up the stairwell. Closing her eyes, she listened to him straighten up the kitchen. Put away her sweater and boots. Fill the teakettle.

Then the front door opened and she heard him rustle with something. Then she heard him mumble something to himself. And then only silence.

That got her to her feet.

Slowly, she descended the stairs, wondering what he could have found outside the front door. Perhaps it was a package? She certainly hadn't expected one.

Ben looked up when she came into view. "Hey, Judith. I was about to come find you."

"You were?" She noticed that he was holding an envelope. "What is that, Ben?"

"It's a note from Bernie. When I opened the front door to get the paper, I saw it. I guess she stopped by here this evening."

"That's a surprise." Only with the greatest effort did she keep her expression neutral as she sat down next to him. Their social worker didn't ever stop by unannounced. She was too busy for that—and besides, that wasn't her way. She was an extremely organized lady. "What does the note say?"

He took a deep breath. "That she needs to talk to us right away. There have been some changes that we need to know about."

"Changes?" She wrinkled her nose. "What is that supposed to mean?"

He looked at the note again. "She doesn't say. All she does say is that she needs to speak with us tomorrow. That she'll plan to be here sometime before noon. And that if we can't be here, to call from our phone shanty and let her know."

Her heart started pounding, as did her head. Actually, she was beginning to feel physically ill. "I wonder what has happened now. Do you think something bad happened?" Reaching out, she clutched his arm. "Ben, what if the social workers have changed their minds about us taking care of James? Or maybe Kendra did!" Panic set in. "Can she do that? Can they do that? Can people just change their minds, willy-nilly?"

Ben turned and reached for her hands. "Judith, calm yourself. We'll find out in the morning. I'll stay home from the store tomorrow until Bernie stops by. No matter what happens, Judith, I won't make you face it alone."

"I know you won't, Ben. You are so good that way." She tried to smile at him but it took too much effort.

After skimming the note again, he set it on the coffee table. "You can read it if you want, but I've already told you what it said."

"I don't need to read it. But thank you."

He stared at her a long moment. She knew what he was doing; he was preparing himself to watch her become hysterical. To break apart like she had when she'd miscarried their baby in the fall.

But she wasn't going to do that. She wasn't going to make him be the strong one all by himself anymore. "I'm all right, Ben. I promise."

After another moment, he nodded. "Are you ready to go to bed? We should probably get some sleep if Bernie is going to come over in the morning. We might need all our wits about us," he said with a small smile.

"You go ahead. I'm afraid I won't be able to sleep for a while."

His smile faded. "Judith, please don't think the worst."

"I won't. I'm simply not tired."

"Judith."

"It's true. I took a little nap with James earlier. *Gut naught.*"

She heaved a sigh of relief when he finally turned away and started up the stairs. She needed some time alone. She didn't have the energy to try to pretend that she wasn't worried sick and on the verge of tears.

And she was so tired of being weak and sad. It was better if he thought she was handling things better than she was.

Something terrible was about to happen; she could feel it in her bones, and it was threatening to destroy her.

"Why, Lord?" she whispered into the silence surrounding her. "Why me?"

It seemed she hadn't been praying hard enough for the Lord's strength. At the moment, it was all she could do not to fall completely apart.

chapter four

Randall had never called a family meeting, but he figured there was a first time for everything.

He was barely able to contain his impatience as Junior and Miriam wandered in, Beverly and her husband, Joe, on their heels. Though it was obvious Randall was waiting for everyone to get settled, Junior and Beverly took their time chatting with Neil and Micah as if they hadn't just seen everyone for Sunday supper.

Five minutes later, Claire and her husband blew in. "I hope this is important, Randall," she said by way of greeting. "Jim and I had quite a time finding a driver on such late notice."

Since when did he have to justify himself? He wasn't the one who moved out to Charm. "I appreciate your efforts to get here. Especially since this is the first time I've ever asked you to come over here for a meeting."

Claire raised her brows at his snippy tone. "Have you made any *kaffi*?"

Like he had time to play host. "I have not."

"Well, I'm going to go make some."

"Claire, we don't need any *kaffi*."

"I do." As she walked to the kitchen, Randall watched her commandeer Levi. "What's going on with Randall?" she whispered not too quietly.

"I don't know," Levi replied. "I just got here."

"Hmm."

He paced impatiently while Claire made coffee, Miriam placed snickerdoodles and brownies on a plate, and Kaylene showed everyone the new book she was reading.

At last, when everyone was sprawled out over the two couches and floor of their great room, Junior looked at him expectantly. "Not that I'm not happy to see everyone, but I'd kind of like to get things started. Miriam and I had other plans for tonight."

Randall did not roll his eyes. But it took effort. Honestly, ever since Junior had suddenly decided that Miriam Zehr was the girl for him, it was like he'd forgotten that he'd spent almost ten years before that completely oblivious to her love for him.

Now he was as smitten as a teenager in the throes of his first crush. To make matters worse, he didn't even seem to care who knew it.

"Randall?" Neil murmured. "Do you want to tell everyone what Levi did or shall I?"

Levi stood up. "Neither of you need to speak for me. I'm old enough to speak for myself, remember?"

"Believe me, we remember," Randall snapped. "Actually, if you are so eager to reveal what you did, go ahead."

Levi's muscles tensed, then he shook his head in obvious exasperation. "All I did was go visit Elizabeth Nolt today."

Looking around the room, Randall was almost pleased to see that everyone in the room was having the same reaction that he'd had when he first heard. Claire and Beverly grimaced. Even Junior looked shocked. And Micah also looked vaguely uncomfortable.

"And why did we need to know this?" Junior asked.

"Give him a minute," Randall snapped. "I'm sure he's getting to it."

After shushing her husband, Miriam spoke. "Did you have a reason for paying her a call, Levi?" she asked. As usual, her sweet demeanor served to put a positive spin on things.

"*Jah*, I had a reason. I offered her a job."

Miriam's eyebrows popped together. "Doing what?"

"Cooking for us. Helping with Kaylene. Laundry."

"You had no right to go out hiring women," Randall said. "Especially not my former girlfriend."

"I live here. That gives me the right."

"It doesn't give you the right to be rude."

"Stop arguing," Junior ordered. "Now, Levi, what did Elizabeth say?"

"She's agreed to come over tomorrow and cook supper."

"Really?" Neil's slim, wiry body visibly relaxed. "That is wonderful."

"*Wunderbaar*," Micah murmured under a faint smile.

To Randall's dismay, everyone in the room looked pretty pleased. "No. No, it definitely is not wonderful," he blurted. "Actually, it's a disaster."

Junior's blue eyes—eyes the exact shade as Levi's and their mother's—narrowed. "Why?"

"Because I don't want her here."

"You don't want her here but I do," Levi countered. "Randall, we need some help. If you weren't so hardheaded you'd see that."

"What made you decide to ask Elizabeth, of all people?" Junior asked. "I mean, I would have never thought of asking her for help."

"A lot of reasons. I like her. Kaylene does, too. I'm sick of chicken and baked potatoes." He lowered his voice. "Plus, I heard through the grapevine that she's having money trouble."

Beverly's husband, Joe, leaned forward, balancing his

elbows on his knees. "She is? What's wrong? Does she need some help with her bills or something?"

"She didn't say," Levi replied. "But I think it does kind of make sense. Remember, her *mamm* got remarried and moved to Pennsylvania. Now it's just her and her grandmother."

"But surely her *mamm* didn't leave them high and dry."

Levi shrugged. "I suppose there's a story there. But like I said, it's only a rumor. Though she was trying to plant vegetables when I got over there."

"She must be having trouble, then. She's a horrible gardener," Randall said. "I've never known Elizabeth to keep a houseplant alive."

Junior looked from Randall to Levi to Neil and Micah. "It sounds like most of you are okay with what Levi did. Kaylene, what do you think about Elizabeth coming over to help out?"

Kaylene shrugged.

Junior studied her a moment, then walked over to crouch in front of their little sister. "Tell me the truth."

"I don't want her here. I want Miriam."

Randall inwardly winced. Even though he hadn't wanted Elizabeth, he'd hoped that Kaylene's outburst the other night had been a onetime thing.

After exchanging glances with his wife, Junior said, "Kaylene, do you want to move in with Miriam and me?"

Her eyes widened. "You two live in a house near Main Street. Not here on our farm."

"That's true. But it's kind of fun living near everything."

Randall held his breath. Until that very moment, he hadn't completely realized just how much it would hurt to let Kaylene go. He would not only feel like he'd failed her, but he'd also miss her.

Kaylene, with her purple and pink dresses, hugs, and constant chatter, made their house a home. If she left, it would feel like he and his brothers were simply biding their time until something better came along.

After seeming to seriously consider the option, Kaylene shook her head. "I don't want to leave. I like living here."

"We like having you here with us, little sister," Neil said gently. "Micah, Randall, Levi, and I might not do things the same way as Junior, but I promise, we love you just as much."

The expression on their little sister's face spoke volumes. That had been just what she'd needed to hear.

As Randall gazed at her, he felt a lump in his throat. Why hadn't he realized that Kaylene had needed a little more attention now that Junior and Claire and Beverly were out of the house?

Why hadn't he told her that she was loved more often? He would have thought he would have instinctively done that. Everyone knew little girls needed lots of care and reassurance.

Swallowing his pride and all of his doubts, he said, "Kay, why don't we see how things go with Elizabeth? She is a mighty nice woman. So kind, too."

"And she sure can make a good cherry pie. Almost as good as yours, Miriam," Levi said with a wink.

Miriam chuckled. "I've obviously been neglecting my new siblings. I'll start bringing over more treats."

Just as Randall had started to relax, Kaylene's eyes teared up. "Why can't things be like they used to be?"

"Because that isn't the way life is supposed to be," Junior said. "The Lord depends on us all to grow and change. Nothing stays the same. Not even you."

She blinked. "I haven't changed!"

"Sure you have! You used to be a little tiny thing. We used

to have to carry you about the house like a sack of potatoes," Junior teased.

"I remember when you used to be afraid of the dark," Randall said. "And when you used to sing nursery rhymes around the house."

"I remember when you liked pretending you were a kitten," Neil said with a smile. "One time I had to put your milk in a saucer so you could lap it up."

"I never did that."

"Oh, yes you did," Neil retorted with a laugh. "You, my sister, didn't just like animals, you wanted to be one."

Miriam got to her feet and held out her arms. After Kaylene walked into her embrace, she said, "And I remember how you used to not be able to read. Now you read circles around us all."

When Kaylene stepped out of Miriam's embrace, Randall strode over and swung her up into his arms. "Please don't worry, little sister," he whispered into her ear. "I won't let you down. I promise you that."

When her spindly arms hugged him right back, Randall made himself a promise. No matter what, he was going to make sure he didn't let her down again.

She was too important to him. Too important to them all.

Lizzy, you are a *wonderful-gut* girl, but I'm just not sure if you should be going over to the Beilers. Especially not to cook and clean for them."

"There's nothing wrong with cooking and cleaning, Mommi. It's honest work."

"Perhaps, but it seems like a fairly good way for you to get your heart broken, if you ask me."

Her grandmother was one of the smartest people Elizabeth knew. She was probably right about her warning. But it couldn't be helped. Getting hired by the Beilers was the best chance she had for keeping a roof over their heads.

And the fact of the matter was that she was willing to do anything to keep her grandmother happy. Even be around Randall. "Mommi, my heart isn't in danger of being hurt," she lied. "I'll be okay."

To Elizabeth's dismay, her grandmother shrugged off her statement. "Why are you going over there, really? Is it to help the Beiler boys eat better? Or is it because you still aren't over Randall?"

There were a lot of reasons. It was because they really, really needed some extra money. It was because it pleased her to do something well that could help others. And for her, that was what cooking and crafting did. She liked doing things for other people—and she was also just vain enough to know that she appreciated being thanked for her efforts, too.

She also wanted to see Randall again, in a way that wouldn't be filled with pressure or false expectations. If Levi hadn't been exaggerating, if things really were in disarray at his house, it meant that Randall had been telling her the truth when he said they couldn't see each other again.

And if that was the case, she knew she owed him an apology. If she was honest with herself, she knew there had been times when she'd dismissed his concerns when he'd confided how much his new responsibilities weighed on him. There had been a few times she'd given him the cold shoulder when he'd been late or forgotten about a date altogether because of a family obligation. Sometimes, she'd even ignored his excuses, thinking he would have tried harder to spend time with her . . . if that had been what he'd really wanted.

"It's a lot of things. And *jah*, I do want to see Randall, Mommi. I fear I misjudged him when we broke up. And, well, the extra money would be nice."

"We should write to your mother and tell her that she needs to send more money."

"I'm not going to do that."

"Just because she has started a new family, it don't mean that she can forget about you."

"She hasn't." Elizabeth feared it was more a case of out of sight, out of mind. She was reluctant to say that, however, because it would only highlight the fact that her mother hadn't come back to Sugarcreek to visit in almost eight months. That was double the amount of time in which she'd vowed to return.

Mommi clasped her hands together. "Maybe there's something I could do? I don't move as quickly as I used to, but I'm not completely useless. Not yet, anyway."

"You do enough. You've done plenty all my life. I want to help you, Mommi. I promise, I'm looking forward to going to the Beilers'."

"As much as you'd be looking forward to getting a tooth pulled."

Because that was true, she hid a smile. "Please don't worry. I'll take care of you."

Her grandmother looked like she was tempted to argue, but at last nodded. "Off you go, then. If we keep talkin' you won't get there."

"That is true. I'll be back in a few hours."

"Take your time, dear. I actually have some plans for today."

"Oh?"

"Martha Kempf is going to pick me up and take me to the Sugarcreek Inn for some lunch and a slice of pie."

Elizabeth smiled. Her grandmother didn't get out much, and with their finances being what they were, meals out were few and far between. "That's mighty nice of her."

"I'm looking forward to spending some time with Martha, but I think she's got an ulterior motive." Her eyes twinkled. "Now that her daughter Christina married Aden and they're living in town, she doesn't get to see them much."

"But Christina's still working as a server at the restaurant?"

"She is. The new owner, Pippa Reyes, is doing a bang-up job, I heard."

"I've heard that, too. Have you met Pippa yet?"

"Nope, but I'll fill you in when I see you later."

"I'll look forward to hearing the latest news," she replied, and realized she meant every word. It was going to be a pleasant change of pace to think about someone other than herself.

Or Randall.

Or how she felt about Randall.

"See you later, Mommi. I better be on my way."

"Chin, up, dear. And don't forget, the Lord is always looking out for us. Always."

Bracing herself, Elizabeth picked up her basket and walked out the door. She had no idea what was about to happen. All she could hope for was that the Lord would be watching over them all.

If there was ever a time in her life for extra-special prayers, this was surely it.

chapter five

For the first time since they'd met, Judith didn't smile when she let Bernie inside the house. When she noticed that their social worker looked a little less amiable than usual, Judith feared her worst fears had come true.

As they walked into the sitting room, it was taking everything she had in order not to cry.

But good manners still needed to be observed. "May I bring you some *kaffi*, Bernie?"

"I'd love some, but let's wait a minute." Reaching out, she clasped Judith's hand. "I'm sorry about coming over here on the spur of the moment like this. I have to tell you, I debated for quite some time about leaving you that note. I didn't want to write everything down in a note, but I know my message was pretty cryptic. I'm sorry if you and Ben worried all night."

So far, Bernie's speech had only elevated Judith's worries. Looking over her shoulder, Judith breathed a sigh of relief as Ben walked in to join them. "Ben, is James all right now?"

"He's *gut*."

"Was he sick?" Bernie asked.

"Not exactly." With an amused expression he said, "That boy was up with the roosters this morning. He got cranky pretty early today. He's taking a morning nap." He smiled slightly at Bernie. "*Gut matin*."

"Good morning," Bernie said as she fished in her voluminous tote bag for her notes and slipped her ever-present reading glasses off the top of her head and onto her nose. "There's no good way to say this, so I'm just going to put it out in the open. Kendra has just been diagnosed with colon cancer."

Judith felt like she'd just had the wind knocked out of her. All night she'd been worried about herself and her wants. Never had she stopped to be concerned for Kendra's health. "She has cancer?"

"Yes. I guess she didn't bounce back quite as well as everyone thought after having James. She's got some vitamin deficiencies. And there are some other issues. . . ." She looked at them both over her glasses. "Some of this is private and not to be shared. But what I'm trying to say is that her health is not good. Actually . . . the cancer is stage four. It's progressed far. The doctors fear that it's already traveled to other organs, too." Taking off her glasses, she rubbed her eyes. "Actually, it's a miracle that she was able to have a baby."

"I feel so sorry for Kendra. Is there a chance she will recover?"

After a pause, Bernie said, "Of course, there's always a chance. But the doctors think Kendra's chances are very slim. What we need to concentrate on, unfortunately, is that there is a very good chance that Kendra won't recover."

Ben shifted. "But can't prisoners get chemotherapy or something?"

"Her condition might be too far gone." She pursed her lips. "But that isn't the only reason I came here. I'm afraid there's more."

"More?" Judith clasped her hands together. "What else has happened?"

"Her two sisters were notified about her situation, and I'm

afraid that they are now interested in adopting James. I believe they have also reached out to James's father."

Judith bit her lip to keep from protesting the sisters' decision. Inside, however, she was practically screaming. Especially since they'd already gone down this road once before, and the sisters had decided to leave things how they were.

"But James's father has been out of the picture, right?"

Bernie's expression remained grim. "I had thought so. But if Kendra dies, it changes everything. The courts will have to give the baby the opportunity to get to know his real father and his birth mother's family."

Judith's spirits sank even lower. Just when she'd begun to feel like her life was settled, it felt as if the rug had been pulled right out from under her.

"So what happens now?" Ben asked after glancing at Judith. "And what does this all mean to us? Do Kendra's sisters want to pay us a visit?" His eyes widened. "Will James's father visit us, too? Is he dangerous? What will Kendra think about that?"

"Let's take things one step at a time," Bernie said. "For the moment, everything stays the same. Kendra has begun her battle against her disease, and she's very strong-willed. So there is a hope."

"And if she doesn't survive?"

"Then I have a feeling James's future will be in the hands of a judge. And while he or she is determining what to do with James, it's very likely the judge might ask for James to be raised in a different environment."

Judith could no longer hold her peace. "But Kendra chose us," she sputtered. "We went there and talked to her and she signed the papers," she said in a rush. "And we've taken James to visit Kendra two other times since then."

"I know that."

"But . . . but, that has to mean something. You said it did."

"Your actions say a lot. And Kendra's opinion means a lot, too. It certainly does carry a lot of weight. But she hasn't chosen you to be her son's adoptive parents. She chose you as foster parents."

"It's one and the same," Ben said. "Right?"

"Not in the eyes of the courts."

"Sounds like you're splitting hairs," Ben said. "Bernie, I don't want to sound ungrateful for all your efforts on our behalf, but it suddenly sounds like you're not on our side."

"You forget that I'm always on James's side. That said, I want you to know that I care about you, too. I am on your side." With a sigh, she pulled her glasses off the bridge of her nose and peered at them both. "I am merely trying to prepare you for what might happen. I want you both to be informed."

Looking at Bernie closely, Judith suddenly realized that the social worker was just as sad and rattled by the recent turn of events as they were. "This is hard for you, too, isn't it?"

Bernie nodded. "I'm going to be honest with you. I've been doing this job a long time. I like to think that the reason I've been so good at a difficult job like this is that I've been able to keep a healthy distance. To remain professional. But that hasn't been the case with you or with Kendra and James. I've become emotionally involved with all of you."

She inhaled, took a deep breath, and pushed a chunk of unruly hair off her brow. "I'd love nothing more than to wave a magic wand and make everything work out the way we want them to. But we have to do things the correct way. For James."

The gentle reminder of who they needed to all focus on

helped Judith remain calm. "It sounds like we need to go pay Kendra a visit then."

"That would be the best thing. Unfortunately, she's too sick to receive visitors."

"Is she in her cell?" Judith hated to think Kendra was so sick behind bars.

"She's in the infirmary, but I think it would be best to wait a bit to visit."

"We have to do something, Bernie," Ben said.

"I agree. How about this? I'll start filing paperwork for you all, asking for custody. Meanwhile, you write her a letter. Tell her you talked to me and ask her to send word when she can have visitors. Or, at the very least, can talk on the phone."

"That's it?" It sure didn't seem like much. It certainly didn't seem like enough.

"That's it, for now." She closed her folder and stuffed it inside her tote bag. "Remember, nothing is settled until the judge says so. And that's a ways away. Don't worry about things that haven't happened yet. Doing that will only get you in trouble," she said wryly. "I promise, I've learned that the hard way."

When she stood up, Judith and Ben stood up, too. "Thank you for explaining everything so well."

Bernie grinned, then hugged her tight. "I know this is hard. I know you are feeling confused and a bit at sea, too. But I promise, I'm doing the best I can."

Ben shook his head. "There's no reason for you to say that. We know you are doing your best. And I know the Lord is looking over us, too. What will be, will be. I have faith in that."

Only later, after Bernie had driven off and Ben had gone to the store . . .

After James had woken from his nap and after they'd played blocks on the floor . . .

Did Judith dare let her guard down? Only then did she dare to let her mind drift to that very dark place where she'd lived after her miscarriage.

And wondered how in the world she was going to be able to survive another big loss.

chapter six

As Randall sat on the stoop of the front porch and watched Elizabeth Nolt walk up their long driveway, he gave thanks for small favors. Since he was the only person at home at the moment, no one would catch him staring at her.

He was glad about that, because, well, it was almost impossible for him not to stare.

Seeing Elizabeth walk up to the house, like he'd seen her do countless times before, brought up so many memories. Some were sweet, filled with smiles and laughter, times when they'd been at their best, like when they would joke about his love for all things sweet or her inability to let even her crankiest hen become Sunday supper. At those moments, Randall had been sure that they were experiencing only the first of many happy days together.

Other times were far more difficult to remember, though the memories were as crystal clear as the summer sky. Like every couple, they'd had their fair share of petty arguments. Once, she had gotten miffed because he'd gone on a hunting trip over her birthday. Another time, he'd gotten upset when he'd thought she'd been a bit too friendly with a couple of guys in their circle of friends.

But even those disagreements hadn't lasted all that long, and their moments of making up had always been especially sweet.

Of course, all of that was now in the past.

As Randall continued to watch her, he frowned. The last time they'd been together, he'd been the one walking up her drive.

She'd had on a blue dress and she'd looked beautiful.

He'd been so nervous and worried about breaking up with her, he'd done it in the clumsiest of ways. And then she'd tried not to cry before he rushed out, almost emotionless. But inside he'd felt lower than a cockroach.

To his embarrassment, his eyes had watered as he'd made his way back home. Oh, he'd pretended it was the cold wind that spurred his tears, but he knew better. He'd been as heartbroken as she was.

He'd also been carrying an added measure of guilt.

Now, he could make out her features as she came closer; her pretty brown eyes, eyes he knew were framed by thick lashes. His body was so tense, he felt as if he were about to spring in anticipation. He didn't know if he could have handled seeing her again if they'd had an audience.

When she was halfway to the porch, he walked out to meet her.

And when only a few yards separated them, he attempted to pretend that everything between them was fine and good. Normal. "Thanks for coming over, Elizabeth. I sure appreciate it. I mean, we all do."

"It's not a problem."

"*Gut.*" Standing there by her side, he felt at loose ends, mainly because he wasn't sure what to do with his hands. Neither shaking her hand nor hugging her like he used to seemed appropriate. Feeling even more uneasy, he stuffed his hands in his pockets.

In response, she folded her arms over her chest.

"I, uh, hope you weren't too taken aback by Levi's visit?"

As if she sensed his discomfort, her lips tilted upward. "I was surprised, of course, but I wasn't upset by what he did. Actually, it would be hard to ever feel that way about Levi. He's a good boy. And he has a good way about him."

"Most of the time, he does." Of course, he hadn't been feeling that way when Levi had told him what he'd done!

"I'm glad he came over. It was an opportune time. I am looking forward to hearing more about the job offer, Randall."

He noticed that her voice was crisp. Businesslike. And her stance was a little rigid. It was all so different from the warm way she used to greet him.

He shouldn't have been surprised, but the difference was chilling. "Ah. *Jah*, it's quite a job, looking after the lot of us." He paused, waiting for her to laugh, or to say something about how he wasn't all that difficult.

Instead, she looked at him seriously. Almost as if they were strangers.

And maybe they were now? Had his abrupt change of heart changed her?

"I bet you're chilled." Looking at the sky, he said, "This May weather is such a tease. It looks like it should be warmer than it is."

"May and June are always like that, I suppose. We get fresh flowers and fields of vivid green, but it's never quite warm enough. At least it isn't raining."

"The dry weather has been nice. For sure." Well, they had certainly exhausted that topic. "How about we go on inside now? We'll sit down in the kitchen and talk about everything."

"That sounds *gut*."

When she started toward the house, Randall caught up

so he could walk beside her. Though they'd seen each other from a distance from time to time, he hadn't spent any time with her since that fateful conversation. Now he was unable not to take in every detail about her.

She looked a little thinner. Her eyes were a little more wary. But she still looked as pretty as ever. And, well, he didn't know how she did it, but Elizabeth always smelled like clean laundry and cherries. Sweet and clean and mesmerizing.

As they walked through the entryway and passed the front living room and into the kitchen, Elizabeth seemed to be taking in every square foot. With every step, she looked to be a little more apprehensive.

Immediately, he noticed the dust bunnies in the corners of the woodwork, the stains on the floor, and the fingerprints on the doors. "Try not to look at everything too closely or you'll run away from here as fast as you can!" he joked. "I know it's a mess."

"No, I was just thinking that it sure seemed quiet around here. Who else is home?"

"No one. Just me."

"Oh."

Was it his imagination, or did she now seem even more disconcerted? "Elizabeth, is that all right with you? I mean, you don't mind that it's just me and you for now, do you?"

"Of course not. I'm simply surprised. Where is everyone? I guess Kaylene is still at school?"

"Yep. And Neil is at the feed store. Micah is with a college counselor, and Levi is at his part-time job with the construction firm who hired me." He pursed his lips. "Things are a lot different now that Junior, Claire, and Beverly are married."

"I imagine so. But the three of them are happy, right? I mean, they've looked happy whenever I've seen them around town."

"Oh, *jah*. They're happy as clams." Mentally, he winced. Hopefully he didn't actually sound as bitter as he feared he did.

She sat down on one of the barstools against the island. He decided to keep a safe distance and stood in front of the stove on the island's other side.

"Is this what you do now? Stay here, holding down the fort?"

"So to speak. I don't know if Levi told you, but I cut my hours way back at my construction job."

"I did hear that, though I'm not sure if it was from your brother. I must say I'm surprised. I thought you really liked it."

"I did."

"But?"

"But someone had to spend more time around here. And since it's obvious to all that Micah will one day follow his own path among the Englischers, that person should be me." He shrugged. "I don't mind working only two days a week, but sometimes I fear I'm only making things worse around here. Lately, all I seem to be doing is cleaning and cooking, and none of it very well." As soon as he heard his words, he ached to take them right back. Could anyone sound more pathetic?

And, well, he sounded like a liar, too, since he'd just noticed that one of the saucepans from last night's supper was still on the stove. Inside, the leftover beans no one had wanted had hardened like glue. Hoping she didn't notice it, he hastily picked it up and placed it in the sink.

Eyes following the pan, she murmured, "Even with only five people in the *haus*, I'm sure there's a lot to do."

"There is, and to make things worse, I fear I'm a terrible housekeeper, Elizabeth," he admitted. He gazed at her face, hoping she would either kid about his ineptitude or say that so far, the house didn't look too bad.

But instead, she looked at him in such a steady way that he felt she could see into his soul. After a couple of seconds, she sighed. "What is going on, Randall?"

"Nothing. We simply need some help." Suddenly noticing how the countertops had crumbs from the morning's toast, he attempted to brush them onto a rag.

"Randall, please stop."

"I'm only trying to clean up for you."

"That's why I'm here, *jah?*"

"Not today though."

Her lips curved up. "I promise, I'm not bothered by toast crumbs or dirty pots and pans. Don't clean right now, please? Your jumping around is making me nervous." She gestured to the other stools. "Now, come sit down and tell me what you'd like me to do while I'm here."

"Cook supper. Clean. And then there's also Kaylene."

Elizabeth started to lean against the counter, but then gazed at the wood and Formica top, and seemed to think the better of it. "What about Kaylene?"

"Well, she's at an impressionable age, you know. And she's missing Junior. You remember how close they were."

"He didn't want her to live with him?"

"He offered, but she didn't want to leave. And to be honest, I don't think I can let her go, Elizabeth. She needs to stay here. This is her home. Our home. I need to make things work for her. I'm really worried about Kay."

Her gaze was searching. "So you agreed to me being here because of *Kaylene?*"

He was tempted to shake his head. To tell her that of course it wasn't just about Kay. It wasn't even just about having a dirty house. It was because of everything. His siblings, the house, the changes. Him. Her.

But of course he couldn't say anything like that, because his life hadn't changed. Besides, she needed money, too. "It's everything."

"And there wasn't any other woman in Sugarcreek who you thought could assist your family?"

"I'm sure there are other women who could help us out, but not so many that Kaylene trusts." He ached to say more. But he feared that nothing could come of bringing up old wounds. "Is being here—and being around me—going to be a problem, Elizabeth? I know we didn't end things on a good note."

"Randall, *we* didn't end things. *You* did. You told me that you didn't want to see me anymore. That we couldn't work things out."

He'd been lying, however. He *had* wanted to see her. But he had also wanted to do the right thing for his family. Duty had prevailed.

She looked at him a moment longer, then with a sigh, hopped off the stool. After opening up a couple of cabinets, she pulled out a mug. Then, to his embarrassment, she walked to the stove, grabbed the teakettle, and carried it to the sink.

"I can make you tea, Elizabeth."

"*Nee.* I would like to do it, I think." After vigorously scrubbing last night's pan, she took off the top of the kettle, peeked inside, and frowned. And then started scrubbing the inside.

"I didn't think the inside of a kettle ever needed to be cleaned," he murmured.

"That is obvious." She smiled slightly. "Randall, if you are truly interested in hiring me, I think I need to know more. What will this job entail?"

"How about I help you while we talk, Beth?" When she glared at him over her shoulder, he knew why. He used to call her Beth late at night when he would walk her home. It had been his pet name for her—liking it because no one else ever called her that.

"Randall, can we please discuss the job now?" Her voice was now tinged with stress, and he knew it was all his fault.

The job. Not them. The job. Not how much he'd hurt her. Or the way he couldn't seem to stop staring at her.

He forced himself to think of things in a clear way, to not get emotional. Or to focus on the faint thread of guilt that was needling him, reminding him of how many things she had been doing without.

"After Levi, ah, jumped the gun, we had a family meeting and decided that we do really need to hire someone to come in a few days a week," he said as he watched her rinse the kettle with cool water and then fill it once again. "Since you have been taking care of your grandmother a lot, we thought of you. I mean, Levi did."

"What about the pay?"

Though it was awkward, he pushed through. "We were thinking to pay ten dollars an hour? Would that be sufficient?"

She nodded solemnly. "I think that would be just fine. Now, when would you pay me?"

"I hadn't thought that far ahead. When would you like to be paid?"

"Once a week?" she asked as she set the kettle on to boil. "Would that work all right for you?"

Knowing she needed her pay every week made him feel guilty. They had so much and she obviously did not. "Of course that's fine."

"*Danke.*"

As he watched her shoulders relax, Randall took care to keep his expression neutral. "Elizabeth, would you like an advance or something? Or some money? Do you need some money?" Thinking quickly, he said, "I've got about two hundred dollars in my wallet—"

"I don't need any handouts, Randall. I'm not a charity case."

"You know I don't think of you that way. But we are friends, and friends help each other out from time to time."

"And ten dollars an hour should be fine."

Realizing that she was going to have to work ten hours in order to earn a hundred dollars, he felt pretty cheap. "You know what? Maybe we should raise it to twenty an hour."

"I don't think so. That would be too much."

When the kettle started whistling, he sagged in relief. This had been the most difficult conversation he'd had in some time. Reaching out, he pulled it off the burner.

He was about to offer her tea when she put a peppermint tea bag in her cup and poured the water. "Do you want tea for yourself, Randall?"

"No. *Danke.* You know I don't drink tea."

"Well, you didn't used to. But I thought, perhaps, that might have changed, too."

Unable to wait any longer, Randall said, "What happened to us, Elizabeth? I know I told you that I couldn't see you for a while."

"*Nee*, you told me that you couldn't see me *anymore*. You broke things off."

"Yes, but you seemed to accept it fairly easily."

She inhaled sharply. Looking extremely affronted, she glared at him and said, "It wasn't my place. You are the man."

"You knew I cared. You knew I had plans for us." Remembering all the times they'd gone walking in the fields by her house, holding hands, sneaking kisses. Of course he'd cared! How could she have doubted it?

But instead of softening her stance, Elizabeth looked even more irritated. "I did not, Randall. You never said anything beyond some thinly veiled promises."

He remembered those moments differently. "I said plenty."

"No, you *kissed* me plenty."

He'd done a lot of things wrong, but he knew he hadn't misjudged her responses to him. "Oh, don't act like you didn't like kissing me, too. We both know I treated you respectfully."

"All I really knew was that after two years of courting, after two years of listening to vague promises, you pushed me away with little more than a fond good-bye."

"I only pushed you away because you didn't understand how little time I had to give you. I know I hurt your feelings, but I wish you would at least try to forgive me. You have no idea what it's like to live in a house with so many siblings depending on you."

"That's right. I only know what it's like to live with a grandmother depending on me."

He felt his cheeks burn, but he wasn't exactly sure if it was from embarrassment or frustration.

He feared it was a little bit of both.

"I don't know what you want me to say," he murmured after he settled down. "Before I broke things off, we hardly ever got to see each other anyway. I knew you were upset about it, too. Every time I told you that I couldn't see you, you acted like I was being sneaky and devious."

"I only complained about your lack of time because you gave me no option." Her voice became stronger. "Don't you remember? We would have plans and then you wouldn't show up. Or instead of spending the afternoon together you'd come over for ten minutes and a hasty kiss."

"You're making me sound like the worst sort of boyfriend."

She pursed her lips, not even trying to refute what he said. "You know what happened as much as I do, Randall. You pushed me aside with little explanation, expecting me to accept your decision without argument."

He wanted to gape at her. Ached to argue, to point out the inconsistencies in her argument. He feared if he did that, however, he'd have to admit that he had just as many flaws.

And then, there they would be, rehashing everything that he'd thought a hundred times but had never had the time or the courage to tell her.

Instead, he held his tongue. "Perhaps we should keep our conversation centered on this job after all. I thought I'd show you the house and let you know where everything is in the kitchen."

"There is no need, Randall," she said as she followed him back to the front door. "I know where everything is, heaven knows I've been here enough. All you need to do is leave me in peace and I'll take care of the rest."

Her rejection stung. Though, of course, it always had stung. Knowing he was just as much at fault didn't help him any, either.

Taking care to keep his voice matter-of-fact, he said, "Kaylene will be home at three o'clock. Can you stay until four today?"

"I can."

"In that case, I'll be in the barn. Come get me if you have any questions." And because he'd done it before, he turned around and walked away.

Leaving them both with a lot of questions and no easy answers.

chapter seven

The moment Randall turned his back, Elizabeth walked into the wide entryway of his house and slumped against the wall, almost knocking down the black-and-white building-block quilt hanging above her head.

Taking a quick step to the side, she exhaled and tried to regain her composure. But it was hard.

Randall Beiler irritated her like no one else. He also made her say and do things she knew she should be embarrassed about. And she *was* embarrassed. She hated arguing with him. She hated that she didn't seem able to push her hurt to one side and move forward.

But most of all, she hated remembering how he used to gaze at her so sweetly, as if she were the only girl in the world. Well, the only girl in the world he was interested in.

Remembering some of the things he'd said, fearing that some of his excuses might even make sense, she took another fortifying breath and brushed off her disappointment. Tonight, when she was back home in her quiet house, she would have all the time she needed to dwell on their past.

Now, though, she needed to swallow her pride and do what she could for his family. Now that Randall was gone, she was able to relax enough to really examine the kitchen. She'd only been scrubbing the kettle to have something to do besides stare at him. And maybe to needle him a bit because she was feeling so uneasy being around him again.

As she returned to the kitchen, she realized that under the dirt and grime was the saddest sight ever. Instead of colorful chaos, the large kitchen was spotless and bare. No papers or notes were attached to the front of the refrigerator, nothing lay on the countertops.

She blinked, remembering when Beverly, Claire, and Junior were still in the house. Back then, things had looked much different. The colorful dish towels that used to hang on the gas stove's door handle were now gone. As was the ceramic cookie jar fashioned in the shape of a dachshund.

A year ago, books and papers and candles littered the countertops, making the big house into a comfortable home, illustrating to one and all that a family lived there. Now? What wasn't covered in dust and grime looked sterile, almost as if no one had lived there for months.

Opening the refrigerator, Elizabeth half expected it to be empty and bare, too. Bracing herself, she peered inside, wondering how she was going to make a decent supper out of nothing. But instead of vacant shelves, there was a bounty of food nestled inside. Rows of vegetables, cartons of fresh berries, and a container of raw chicken were on one shelf. Milk, eggs, butter, a block of cheddar cheese, and a carton of sour cream lay on another.

After opening a few cabinets, she found sugar and flour, a glass jar filled with rice and a dozen boxes of flavored gelatin.

It looked like supper was going to be made after all.

With Kaylene in mind, she decided on a simple meal of fried chicken, broccoli and rice casserole, and a Jell-O salad. And she would make some sugar cookies, too, because she had a feeling Kaylene would be happy to have a treat when she came home from school.

After wrapping an old dishcloth around her waist, she got to work, taking pleasure in doing such simple things as measuring flour and sugar, then carefully rolling out the dough. She was humming to herself by the time she was cutting neat circles in the dough with the top of a glass.

Once the first batch of cookies were baking, she walked upstairs, peeking in bedrooms and bathrooms.

Funny how she knew each Beiler well enough to guess whose room was whose, just from the quilts on the beds and the small number of items on desks and bedside tables.

Micah was the easiest to spot. He had piles of textbooks on every available space. He also had three spiral notebooks on his desk, an assortment of pencils, each in various need of sharpening, and a calculator tossed on the floor.

His room was also the only one without a quilt. Instead was a neat-looking plain brown bedspread and three pillows. Four pegs lined one wall. Two shirts, one light blue, one green, hung beside a pair of dark blue pants.

Levi's room was the complete opposite. His bed was unmade; clothes, both Amish and English, littered the floor. On his bedside table was a novel and a sports magazine. But there was also a well-worn Bible next to his bed. Unable to help herself, Elizabeth peeked inside.

As she suspected, it was their family's Bible. Both of their parents' names were neatly inscribed at the top of the first page. Elizabeth ran a hand along the leather cover, wondering just how much Levi missed his parents—and how aware his older brothers were of his feelings. She'd always believed Levi to be far more sensitive than he readily let on.

After folding a couple of his shirts and straightening his

sheets, she gathered up a few items that looked especially dirty and put them in a pile in the hall.

Next she wandered into what had to be Neil's room. It was as neat as a pin. On a beautifully crafted cherrywood desk lay a plain, functional calendar. Lists of chores, auctions, and appointments filled each of the calendar's squares.

Next to a heavy-looking bedside table was his bed. It was neatly made, the sheets tucked in with precision. Covering the queen-sized mattress was a beautifully stitched white-on-white quilt in a rose pattern. Running her hand along the worn fabric, Elizabeth smiled, realizing that their mother had probably quilted the piece. She had a vague memory of hearing about how Mrs. Beiler had been a gifted quilter.

The only thing that gave the room any personality was the overflowing laundry basket filled with clothes that smelled of barns and animals.

Not wanting to get too up-close and personal with his smelly laundry, Elizabeth dragged the whole basket into the hall before looking for Kaylene's room.

Seeing a trio of rooms at the end of the hall, she peeked into the first. It was empty except for a pair of twin beds. The walls were painted a cool blue. When she noticed that one wall easily had a dozen pegs, as well as a set of built-in shelves, she knew the room must have belonged to Claire and Beverly. Next to that room was a completely empty bedroom, its white walls and bare wood floor practically begging for company.

Remembering how close Kaylene was to her eldest brother, she could only imagine that the empty room was Junior's. When she opened the last bedroom door, she grinned.

Inside, there was an explosion of pink and white. Kaylene's walls were painted a soft carnation pink and the quilt was a crazy quilt obviously made up of old dresses of Kaylene's. Small dresses hung on hooks on the walls and brushes and pins lay on the desk.

Stuffed animals of all sorts littered the floor and the bed and the soft-looking easy chair in the corner. An oval rag rug lay in the middle of the room. The bright colors of the rags woven together made the rug look festive and cheerful.

Next to her bed was a white table, its sides gently curved and beveled. On its top lay a box of tissues and two books, one of which was *Little Women*.

She had a pile of towels and laundry in the corner of the room.

After adding Kaylene's laundry to the rather large pile in the hall, Elizabeth walked back downstairs. The cookies were done, so she quickly set them on the countertop to cool.

Then she knew it was time to face one last room. Steeling her shoulders, she walked past the living room and the dining room, finally coming to a stop in front of what had to be the master bedroom.

It was silly, but she was reluctant to enter Randall's bedroom. Half of her was afraid to discover some piece of evidence that he'd changed. The other half was afraid to realize that he was still the same man she'd fallen in love with. If he was, she knew she was about to set herself up for another bout of heartache.

Bracing herself, she opened the door and then stood in awe. Instead of a big bed, he had a futon shaped into a couch of sorts. A pair of pillows and a thick quilt, made up of simple squares in greens and blues, lay at one corner. Next to the futon was a heavy-looking easy chair upholstered in gray plaid. A trio of books lay on the floor. A thick area rug lay in the middle of the wooden floor, and a fairly large bookshelf rested in between the two windows. Lining the shelves were books of all kinds, ranging from history to mysteries to religious texts.

There was also the silly wooden train that she'd given him as a Christmas gift the first year they'd dated. Next to it was a red satin ribbon, tied in a clumsy bow.

She'd given it to him with that bright red bow, saying that with that train, he could follow her anywhere in the world.

Reaching out, she gently ran a finger along the satin ribbon. He'd kissed her for the first time after she'd given him that. And had then whispered in her ear that he didn't need a train to follow her, that she had already claimed his heart.

Then, more recently, he'd come to her house and quietly broken her heart.

Pressing her hand to her mouth, Elizabeth backed away. She hated that he'd kept something so special to her.

Hated that he kept that red ribbon.

Without looking for his laundry, she closed his door with a firm snap. It was simply not possible to carry around any shirts that smelled like him. Her work as his maid only went so far.

Running upstairs, she grabbed an armful of laundry, then ran down two flights of stairs like her feet were on fire. She needed to work hard and try not to think about Randall. Try not to remember their two years together. But just as she closed the washing machine's lid, she drew herself up to a halt.

She'd meant to concentrate on Kaylene's needs. Not hers.

She was going to work on making a decent dinner for Levi, who was so tired of eating grilled chicken and potatoes. She was going to remind herself of how handy the money she was earning was going to be. She'd been meaning to concentrate on anything but Randall.

She'd intended to simply think of her time at the Beilers' home as a job. As a way to pay her bills and take care of her grandmother.

But so far, all she'd been doing had been taking a trip down memory lane, dredging up old memories while she did so.

At this rate, she was going to either fall back in love with Randall or be reduced to tears.

chapter eight

Elizabeth had completed three loads of laundry and baked four dozen cookies by the time Kaylene walked through the kitchen door with Neil.

"Hi, Elizabeth," the little girl said with wide eyes. "My brothers said you might be here."

"And I am. It's good to see you." Lifting her head, she smiled at Neil. "Hello, Neil."

Neil's gaze softened. "You are a sight for sore eyes, Elizabeth. Thank you for helping us out. I hope we're not causing too much trouble for you. We Beilers can be kind of a mess."

"Not at all. As I told Randall, I'm happy to be of use. And I was looking forward to seeing all of you again." Well, almost all of them.

"I feel the same way. We lost a *gut* friend when you and Randall broke up." He winced. "I hope you don't mind me sayin' that."

She chuckled. "I've felt the same way." Noticing that Kaylene was still looking at her like she might disappear at any minute, she waved a hand toward the two plates filled with cookies sitting in the middle of the kitchen table. "Would either of you like a cookie? They're just sugar cookies but they're pretty *gut*."

"Asking if we want a cookie is like asking if we would like

the sun to rise, right, Kay?" As his little sister nodded, Neil reached down and plucked one off the table. After biting in, he closed his eyes and groaned in pleasure. "They're still warm. And delicious!"

"*Danke.* I made fried chicken for you, too. And broccoli and rice casserole."

Neil's expression turned to one of bliss. "Can I tell you again that I'm mighty glad you're here?"

Feeling lighter than she had all day, Elizabeth giggled. "You can tell me that as often as you'd like."

After stealing another two cookies, Neil turned to go back out the door. "If you need something, I'll be out in the barn," he said as he strode to the mudroom.

Kaylene was rooted to her spot, still wearing her backpack. She looked like she couldn't decide whether to stay or to run out of the room.

Elizabeth knew that something needed to be said. "Kaylene, I know when I was seeing Randall we never had much of an occasion to talk. But I'd like to get to know you now. Why don't you take off your backpack and sit with me awhile?"

"I'm going to go on up to my room."

"You don't want a snack?"

Kaylene shook her head. "Not right now."

"But couldn't we at least sit together for a little bit? I'd love to hear how your day went."

Kaylene edged toward the door. "I know you're only here because my brothers are paying you."

"That's not the only reason I'm here."

"But it's a job, right? They are paying you to cook and clean? To be our maid."

Hating that she was being reduced to that status when she had always planned to be Kaylene's sister-in-law, Elizabeth nodded. "You're right. I am here to cook and clean. And I am going to be paid for it."

Kaylene's eyes widened, right before they filled with tears. Then, without another word, she turned away and walked upstairs.

Elizabeth was so stunned, she sat down at the kitchen table. She hadn't remembered Kaylene being anything but welcoming and well-mannered when she and Randall had dated. Whenever she'd seen the girl she had always been smiling and happy.

Of course, she'd also been practically glued to Junior's side or helping her sisters around the house. And she'd loved reading with Miriam, too.

Elizabeth now understood what Randall and Levi had meant when they said that Kaylene needed her. It was obvious that she was afraid to trust anyone.

So many people in her life had left her, some through death, others in the normal progression of things. Maybe she was even mourning the fact that so many people in her life had moved on.

Elizabeth could definitely understand that. She'd been difficult in the year after her father passed away. And no one could deny she'd had trouble adjusting to her mother remarrying and starting a whole new family.

She was going to need to do some thinking about how to best reach out to the girl without pushing too hard.

She'd just gone out to the clothesline when Randall came out to meet her.

"Where's Kaylene?"

"Hi, Randall, I'm fine," she replied pertly. "So far everything's going pretty well, thank you for asking."

"Sorry. Hi. Do you know where Kay is?"

"I think she's in her bedroom. She went up there as soon as Neil went out to the barn."

He frowned. "Why did she go up there? Why isn't she here with you? I thought you were going to spend some time with her."

"I tried, but that wasn't what she wanted to do."

Before she could explain her reasoning, tell him that she thought it would be better to take baby steps with Kaylene instead of forcing her presence on the girl, Randall pulled off his hat and rubbed the back of his neck in a move that signaled his frustration. "Elizabeth, didn't you understand that part of the reason we wanted you here was to spend time with Kay?"

"Believe it or not, I did understand that."

"Well, then? What happened? I can't believe you're ignoring her."

"Nothing 'happened.' And I'm certainly not ignoring her."

"What did you do?"

Now completely irritated, she tossed the shirt she was folding into the basket at her feet. "I did nothing wrong. Your sister is hurting. She needs a gentle touch. I will reach out to her, but I don't think now is the best time."

His stance turned obstinate. "But—"

"You need to trust me on this, Randall."

"But—"

Her patience was at its end. "Enough." Picking up the laundry basket, she thrust it into his arms. "I'm going to go home now. If you want me to come back, come see me. Otherwise, send me my pay in the mail."

"What are you talking about? I thought you wanted to be paid on Fridays."

"That's what I said, but I didn't think you were going to be so rude and question everything I'm doing. I need a job, but not this badly."

"All I did was ask why you weren't spending time with my sister."

"You did more than that, and you and I both know it." Suddenly, it was all too much. It was too hard being in the Beiler kitchen as their cook when she'd always imagined it would be hers.

It was hard tiptoeing around Kaylene when she'd thought they were going to be sisters.

And it was almost impossible to be around Randall as his maid when she'd spent two years being so much more. And with that, she turned, walked back to the house, grabbed her things, and started walking down the long driveway.

She didn't care if it took her a whole hour to walk home. In fact, if it did, it would be a whole hour's respite from the Beiler family—and from all the questions her grandmother was sure to ask.

An hour's break from her life sounded like a mighty good thing at the moment.

W as there any scarier time than two in the morning? As Judith tried her best to comfort a crying James, she knew she was starting to dread the middle of the night.

Ever since Bernie had come over and told Judith and Ben the news about Kendra's health, Judith had been besieged by nightmares. She'd practically fall into bed at the end of each day and instantly go to sleep. But then, after only a few hours' rest, all of her worst fears would surface. She'd dream that James's family would knock on their door and take him away. Or that Bernie would snatch him from her arms.

Or that she would do something wrong with James because she wasn't a "real" mother. That was the worst dream of all, because in those she was the one at fault.

After awakening she would find it impossible to sleep. As quietly as possible, she would slip on her robe and slippers and walk downstairs. And then would spend the next hour worrying and pacing.

Tonight, soon after waking from yet another terrible dream, she heard James fussing. Patting his back, she carried him downstairs in the hopes that Ben could stay asleep.

That had been almost thirty minutes ago.

Now, James was still crying and she was near tears, too.

Suddenly, her worst fears felt like her reality. She was a terrible mother. She didn't deserve to be his *mamm*.

"Up again?" Ben asked as he walked into the room.

"*Jah.* I'm sorry we woke you."

Perching on the arm of the couch, he gazed at her in concern. "Have you given him some pain reliever? Remember what your mother said? He's getting his front teeth."

"I haven't yet." Holding up the bottle, she said, "I thought maybe he was hungry."

"I'll get the medicine. It's worth a try, ain't so?"

Closing her eyes, she nodded. And felt the guilt slide over her further. Why hadn't she gotten the pain reliever first thing?

When Ben returned with a dropper of pink liquid, he carefully popped some in the baby's mouth. James swallowed, fussed, then started crying again.

But to Judith's amazement, instead of being worried, Ben only took James from her arms with a chuckle. "You are an unhappy boy tonight, aren't ya?" he cooed.

"I'll go get a cold washcloth from the refrigerator. He liked chewing on that yesterday."

Still smiling, he nodded. "Good idea."

She rushed to the kitchen, got the cold, wet washcloth and handed it to James. The baby clutched it, then brought it to his mouth. Seconds later, a delicious peace settled in the room.

Ben smiled at her. "Success."

"Indeed. At long last."

"He's bound to get sleepy soon. Why don't you go on up to bed, if you think you can sleep now?"

She was tired all of a sudden. "I'll give it a try. Since it looks like you've got everything handled."

His expression sobered. "Judith, don't do this. Don't feel bad about yourself. It takes two of us, remember?"

"I remember. I'm just so afraid about the future."

"I know. I am, too. But it's out of our hands. Remember that old saying? It's a good one. 'Reach up as far as you can. God will reach the rest of the way.' "

She swallowed. "You truly believe that, don't you?"

"I have to." As James cuddled close to him, he murmured, "Miracles do happen to those who believe. I'm living proof."

"And why is that?"

"Because He already gave me you, *mein lieb*. Now, go try to sleep."

For the last year, she'd been a mess of emotions. It had been such a time of highs and lows. Through it all, Ben had been her rock. "Ben, do you have regrets?"

"About you? Not a one," he said with a wink.

"What about us taking in James, even though we might lose him one day? Do you ever wish we'd done things differently?"

"*Nee.*"

He sounded so assured, so certain, she was staggered. "How can you be so sure?" she whispered.

"Judith, tonight when James cried, you were there for him. When he needed comfort, we gave him medicine. When he's been hungry, we fed him, and when he needed to be held and loved, we've done that, too. No matter what the future brings, right now, right this minute, he needs us. And we need him, Judith. He's brought us so much joy and happiness, even for this short amount of time."

"He has, hasn't he?"

Ben nodded. "He's been a blessing. And for me, Judith, that is enough. Isn't it enough for you?"

Mesmerized by his words, she nodded.

An hour later, when she at last drifted off to sleep, her husband's words kept ringing in her ears.

And she finally relaxed and felt at peace. Because having James right now, right this minute, truly was a wondrous gift. "It is enough, Lord," she whispered. "It is definitely enough."

chapter nine

"Welcome to the Sugarcreek Inn," Pippa Reyes said from her position behind the hostess podium located at the very front of the Amish restaurant.

The older gentleman who had just walked in the front door narrowed his eyes. "You're new."

She almost chuckled at the way he was looking at her so cautiously through a thick pair of tortoiseshell glasses. But instead of laughing, she stood still and kept her expression polite and serene.

After all, he wasn't the first person to comment about her presence—or to look at her curiously. She supposed anyone would be caught off guard about a Hispanic woman greeting customers at an Amish restaurant.

But she did wonder what this customer would think if he knew the whole, complete truth about her job description. She wasn't just a new employee; she was also the new owner of the veritable institution. But she didn't think the man wanted to hear about that. "Yes, I am," she said. Noticing that he was with two other men about his age, she picked up three menus. "Do you gentlemen need a table for three?"

"Yeah," he said. "Miss, where are you from?"

"Toledo."

His eyes widened, almost as if she'd told him she'd come from the mountains of Guatemala. "Pretty far."

"Yep." After seating the men at a table, she told them about their specials, then signaled for Christina Reese to bring them some water and coffee.

Making her way back to the hostess station, Pippa bit her lip to keep from smiling. The sad fact was that the man's reaction and comment happened more often than not. It seemed Sugarcreek was not only a small town; it was a very small town. And somewhat of a closed community, too. Anything new was at first looked upon with skepticism. Only then, after everyone stewed about it for a while, did it become embraced.

And that was what she was waiting for, Pippa knew. To be embraced.

In the figurative way, not literal. She was still recovering from an ugly divorce. No way did she want to enter into another relationship anytime in the near future.

When the restaurant's door opened again, Pippa pasted a smile on her face. "Welcome to the Sugarcreek Inn." The rest of her spiel was cut off, because, unfortunately, she knew who had arrived. Bud Hayes. "Hi."

"Hi, Pippa." The lines around his eyes crinkled, matching his easy smile.

She supposed some women might think they were attractive. She did not.

Maybe he didn't notice her silence. Or maybe he did and just didn't care? Whatever the reason, he stepped forward and rubbed his hands together. "It took me forever to warm up my truck this morning. Hard to believe it's May. Feels like February."

She needed to say something. Anything. "Well, it is May."

One eyebrow perked up, making him look almost amused. "I came in for a cup of coffee."

"Then you're in luck," she said lightly. "That's something we happen to have a lot of around here." To cover the nervous flutter in her stomach, she grabbed a menu and led him to one of the two-person tables near the window.

He sat down with a look of pleasure. "Thanks for seating me here. You know how much I like to look outside."

Boy, did she! Even as she told herself she wasn't going to do it, she felt herself flush. Reminding her of what he'd seen out his window the week before she moved out of the small apartment she'd shared with Miguel.

Not ready to dwell on that awful evening, she cleared her throat. "Christina will be over with coffee soon. She'll explain today's pies and specials as well, if you happen to be interested. Have a nice day."

"Wait, Pippa. Can't you stay and talk to me for a minute or two?"

Well, she could, if she wanted to. She did not. "I'm pretty busy, Bud." But she didn't move, which was a good thing, seeing how the dining room was pretty much empty except for the two of them and the table of men that she'd just seated.

"Yeah. I can see that." Blue eyes softened. "Please, Pippa? If you want to know the truth, I didn't come over here for just the coffee."

"Oh?"

"It's pretty obvious I wanted to see you."

Valiantly, she cautioned her heart to ignore both his words and the kind way he was gazing at her. "Bud, I don't know why you'd want to see me again."

"That's why you need to have a seat, don't you think?" he asked lightly. "Pippa, sit down. We really do need to talk."

She didn't want to do this. She didn't want to sit down across from him and relive the last time they'd seen each other. She especially didn't want to do it in the middle of her restaurant.

"Please, Pippa? Can't you spare me a couple of minutes?"

Just as Christina approached, coffee carafe in hand, Pippa sat. "I'm going to have some coffee with an old friend for a minute, Christina. If someone comes in, seat them, would you?"

"*Jah*. Sure, Miss Pippa. *Kaffi* for the both of you?"

After a brief look at Bud, Pippa resigned herself. "Yes, please." And then she remembered something her mother used to say. *In for a penny, in for a pound.* "And bring us two slices of Marla's sour cream coffee cake, would you? It smelled like heaven this morning."

"It tastes like heaven." Christina's light blue eyes widened. "Um, I mean, Marla let us have a little piece."

Pippa smiled. "I'm glad you got to try it."

While Christina darted back to the kitchen, Bud leaned back, crossing his arms over his chest. "So the rumor I heard was true. You really are managing this place."

"I am more than the manager. I am part owner." Of course, the minute she said the words, she wished she could take them back. After all, pride was a sin.

"Miguel didn't tell me that. He'd be impressed."

As she realized he'd gotten all his information from her ex, the little burst of happiness she'd started to feel vanished. "I don't want to talk about Miguel. Or did you come here because of him?"

"I came here in spite of him," Bud retorted before Pippa was able to apologize for her tone. His gaze never left hers as he sipped his coffee. "He would be pretty upset if he knew I was here, talking to you like this."

"Bud, why did you come?"

"So I could ask if you are always going to hold what I saw against me. Are you?"

"I hope not."

"Pippa, me seeing you crying is not the end of the world."

"I wasn't just crying, Bud. We know that." Remembering that day too vividly, her heart felt heavy. It had been only two months after she and Miguel had separated, and the reality of their new situation had finally settled in and hit her hard. As bad as her marriage had been, she'd been part of a couple. Not alone.

She'd felt guilty about getting divorced, especially because her mother didn't believe in divorce and had told her so with increasing fervor.

She'd also been working as many shifts as her manager at the superstore would give her so she could afford both the first and last months of her apartment's rent. All those things combined had made her emotionally and physically exhausted.

On that last evening, she'd tripped and fallen on the pavement. Of course she'd had her purse and two grocery sacks in her arms. Everything in her purse had fallen out—and the plastic sacks had ripped open.

And just like a spark had been lit, she'd burst into tears.

She'd ended up sitting on the bottom step leading up to her second-story apartment and crying like a baby.

Her only solace had been that it was late, it was dark, and no one was around. Then Bud's door opened and he'd met her gaze.

Bud had been Miguel's best friend. Seeing him had practically been an invitation for her ex-husband to find out just how not well she was doing.

"Did you ever tell Miguel about that day?"

"You mean that night?" he corrected gently, just as Christina came over with two plates of coffee cake and a fresh pot of coffee. "Thanks," he said.

"Need anything else, Miss Pippa?"

"I think we're good. I'll just be a few more minutes."

Christina's eyes widened, but she said nothing more, just went to the front of the dining room to greet some customers.

"I should go," Pippa said, knowing she sounded like a fool. After all, she was the one who'd asked for the coffee cake.

"I never said a word to anyone, Pippa," he said quietly.

Remembering how he'd stared at her long and hard before going back into his apartment for a canvas tote, which he used to pick up her groceries—and feminine products!— Pippa felt that helpless embarrassment wash over her yet again. "I still get embarrassed when I think about that night."

"Why? You were getting a divorce, working too much, and all of your groceries had just scattered all over the sidewalk."

She speared a forkful of cake and took a bite, remembering how he'd walked everything up the stairs to her apartment and held out his hand for her keys.

Like a fool, she'd given them to him.

He'd unlocked her door, turned on her light, and set that tote inside. And then, to her astonishment, he'd pulled a handkerchief out of the pocket of his jeans. Who in the world still carried handkerchiefs, anyway?

Then he'd walked back down the stairs. Only later, after she'd dried her tears, put her things away, and settled down with a mug of hot chocolate did she realize that she'd never even thanked him.

"I never thanked you," she blurted. "I never thanked you for helping me pick everything up and carrying it up those stairs. For helping me get inside safely." She shook her head, feeling dismayed again about her rudeness. "For never spouting your opinion about the divorce or peppering me with questions. All you did was hand me that handkerchief."

"I didn't need to be thanked, Pippa. I just wanted to help you."

Staring into his eyes, she finally realized that, too. "That's really all it was, wasn't it? You were simply being kind."

"Is that so hard to believe?"

She averted her eyes. Meeting his gaze was too hard. If she did, she felt like she would have to admit out loud all the mistakes she'd made. "I used to think anyone who was friends with Miguel couldn't be friends with me."

"I hope you change your mind about that." Carefully, he wiped his mouth, then set his paper napkin over his clean plate. "Just because I still talk to Miguel, it doesn't mean I'm just like him."

"Are you sure about that?"

"More than sure." His voice hardened, but not with animosity. Instead, it filled with confidence. "For better or worse, I'm my own man, Pippa. And . . . I hope, in time, you'll see that."

It felt like he was telling her a lot. Like he was trying to let her know something without being obvious. But she wasn't good at that anymore. "I'm not sure what you want."

"I want to get to know you better. I've always wanted to get to know you better."

"You have?"

He nodded, looking a little sad. "I know you need time,

and I'm good with that. I just want the chance to talk to you some. Maybe see you again, when that is something you're comfortable with."

"I see."

"Do you?" His eyes lit up, like he was amused. "In that case, could I have your phone number?"

"No." She closed her eyes, hating how she had the manners of a wild dog or something. "I'm sorry. I mean that I'm just not ready for that. Yet."

"All right, then." Pulling out his wallet, he handed her a twenty-dollar bill and a business card. "Here's my number. I'd love to hear from you." Looking a little sheepish, he added, "I'd even be happy with a text. And here's what I owe you for breakfast."

"This is too much." At that moment, she wasn't sure if she was talking about his phone number or the money.

Getting to his feet, he shook his head slightly. "It's not too much, Pippa." He turned and walked out the door before she could argue with him.

Shaking her head in dismay, she grabbed the twenty and, after a moment's pause, that card.

And as she went to the cash register to put in the bill, she realized that she'd never given him back that canvas tote—or his handkerchief.

Maybe someday soon she'd use that as a reason to give him a call back. Or at least text him.

Maybe someday she'd be brave enough to do that. Maybe.

chapter ten

Mucking out stalls should be a solitary chore. Really. It was a dirty, smelly job, and one that Randall had never especially enjoyed. But the older he got, the more he appreciated it. He could see the results right away, and their horses always seemed a lot happier when they were standing on fresh straw.

But those reasons didn't mean that he wanted to drag the task out longer than necessary.

"I told you I got this, Levi," Randall said under his breath.

"And I told you that taking care of these stalls is my job." With a scowl, he snatched the rake out of his hands. "I promised Junior I would still do it after he left."

It made no sense, but his youngest brother's reminder that Junior's word was still heeded—even though he was living on his own now—grated something awful.

Enough to pick a fight.

"And I told you that I have time, and I don't mind doing it. Let me be and go on to work."

"I don't start my shift until eleven today," Levi said as he neatly ran the rake along the side of the stall, easily picking up more soiled straw in one pass than Randall did in three. "Plus, you aren't doing it right."

"And we both know that there's only one way to clean out a stall."

"There's only one way to do it the way Bright likes."

"She's a horse."

"She's a *gut gaul*. Even I remember Daed saying that we needed to care for her well, because she cares for us," Levi snapped. "Don't you remember that?"

"Of course I do. Daed told me that a whole lot longer ago than you." As soon as the words left his mouth, he wished he could take them back. The reason Levi hadn't heard his father's words of wisdom for as long was because he was so young when their father passed away. "I'm sorry. I shouldn't have said that."

"*Bruder*, what's wrong with you? You're not acting like yourself at all."

Randall immediately felt ashamed. His brother was right. There was no reason for him to be taking out his frustration on a horse's stall anyway. "You're right. I'm sorry."

"You know, if you're upset with the way you treated Elizabeth, you should just go over there and apologize. It might take a while, but I bet you'll find the right words to say to her sooner or later."

"I didn't know you were now in the business of giving advice, *bruder*."

"I'm not. But if you aren't going to be paying a call on Elizabeth, let me know. I'll go over there and apologize."

Against his will, a burst of jealousy hit him hard. "Have you developed a crush on her, Levi?"

Taking a deep breath, Levi rested the rake against the slats of the stall before facing him. "You know, I used to really admire you. Out of all my older brothers, I admired you the best. I liked how you were always so easygoing. I liked how you kept to yourself and worked construction and always had a joke or a smile for me. But now I get it."

"And what do you get?"

"You weren't easygoing; you were selfish. You were happy because you were doing exactly what you wanted, when you wanted. And now that you can't, you don't know how to deal with it."

"That is not true." At least, he really hoped it wasn't.

"It sure seems like it is. If you don't want to be in charge, tell Micah or Neil. Or tell Junior. I bet he'd come back and do everything again. And then you could go back to doing what you wanted."

"Listen to you," he said sarcastically. "You've got all the answers this morning."

"Not really. Because Kaylene is still sad, we're going to have hockey-puck chicken again tonight, and you probably hurt Elizabeth's feelings. She's probably wondering how she's going to be able to take care of her grandmother now." Looking even more irritated, Levi thrust his rake at Randall. "Here, you want to finish up? Go ahead. I'm going to walk Kaylene to school."

"Wait. I haven't made her lunch yet."

Levi rolled his eyes. "I already made it."

"Really?"

"Don't you get it, Randall? As much as you seem to believe you've got the whole family's burdens on your shoulders, you don't. Once more, you never have."

Only when he was alone again did Randall dare admit that his little brother was right. He had always been happy, because he had been thinking only about himself.

And yet again, here he was, thinking only about himself. He was focusing on how much he still wanted Elizabeth in his life. Secretly admitting to himself that he still loved her. But instead of doing something about it, he was behaving like a teenager, finding fault with her instead of himself.

No, he corrected, thinking of Levi and his words, he was behaving worse than a teenager. He needed to go apologize to her as soon as possible.

And, he realized with a sense of dismay, there was no better time than the present.

After all, it seemed that his little brother was taking care of everything else.

Less than an hour later, he was riding his bike to Elizabeth's house. His mind was blank. He truly had no idea how he was going to find the words to apologize to Elizabeth. Or how he was going to be able to convince her to come back to work.

He hoped the Lord would take pity on him by the time he got to her front door and knocked. It was obvious that, left in his hands, things were going to go just as poorly as ever.

"Please, Got, help me out here," he murmured to himself as he knocked, then waited for Elizabeth to answer.

Then was caught completely off guard by her grandmother instead. "*Gut matin*, Anna Mae."

She stepped back to let him inside. "And the same to you, Randall. What brings you by here so early this morning?"

"I was hoping to talk to Elizabeth. Is she here?"

"She is, though I doubt she wants to talk to you."

"I bet she doesn't—which, of course, is the exact reason I need to talk to her."

"Oh?"

Randall was becoming uncomfortably aware that Anna Mae was in no hurry to get Elizabeth—or to let him off the hook. "I messed up things with her yesterday."

"She told me that. Matter of fact, she said she weren't real happy with you." With a look of distaste, she added, "And that your *haus* was a mess."

"Our *haus* is a mess. But I'm hoping to one day get better. And I'm trying to work out things with her, too."

When it was obvious that Anna Mae wasn't the least bit impressed, he shrugged. "I don't know what else I can tell you. It's obvious that I need Elizabeth's help. At least, it is to me."

At last, her eyes sparkled a bit. "Why don't you go take a seat in the kitchen? I'll tell Elizabeth that you've come to grovel."

While she walked down the hall, Randall struggled to keep a straight face. She was exactly right; he'd come to lay his ineptitude in front of her with the hope that she was going to take pity on him.

He wandered into the kitchen. It looked just as it had when he used to come calling. It wasn't a fancy kitchen, but perfectly suited to Elizabeth. She was a unique combination of traditional Amish values with just a splash of modern sparkle.

They'd spent so many evenings simply sitting on the kitchen stools next to the counter sipping hot chocolate, and talking. Being in the room again fairly took his breath away. The walls were painted a butter yellow. The cabinets were old, but had been painted a soft blue. The counters were made of white tile. The floor was highly polished cherry-wood. Pots and pans hung from a large iron holder above the butcher block in the center of the room. All of the pots and pans were stainless steel and sparkled like they'd just come from the store.

He knew, however, that they were years old. Elizabeth merely cared for them just like she did everything else—with a liberal dose of care and love.

And he'd brushed off everything she'd offered with hardly a backward glance.

"Hello, Randall," Elizabeth said as she entered the room, just as if he'd conjured her.

Turning, he smiled. "Hey. I was just looking at everything. You really do have the prettiest kitchen I've ever seen."

"*Danke.* It's my pride and joy."

Fingering one of the pans above his head, he asked, "How do you keep your pans looking so shiny and clean? I can almost see my reflection in them."

"I've got some cleanser called Barkeeper's Friend. That and baking soda seems to do the trick."

"I'll have to give that a try. Ours don't look near as pretty."

"The trick is to take your time. When you scrub too hard, the stainless steel gets scratched."

"Ah."

She smiled softly, making him feel like she'd just given him a hug. "I never thought I'd see the day when we would be talking about cleaning pots and pans."

He shrugged. "I'm starting to realize that a lot of things have happened that I didn't anticipate. It's taught me to keep on my toes."

"That is true. The Lord is certainly in charge, ain't so? He throws things in our carefully organized lives time and again."

"He knows best. But sometimes, well, I wish His lessons weren't always so difficult to learn."

She nodded in agreement, then looked at him closely. "Why did you come over, Randall?"

"I came to grovel. But I would have thought your grandmother would've told you that."

"Um, well, she might have." She pulled out one of the bar stools and sat down primly. "Want to sit down?"

He did, but he feared it would bring back too many memories. "I think it might be better if I stand," he said, hoping she didn't notice just how much he was staring at her. She looked pretty today in a dark blue dress, the color so rich he might have mistaken it for purple. He wasn't sure what it was about her that had always drawn him. Sure, she was pretty, but other girls were, too.

And her thick brown hair and deep brown eyes were attractive, too.

But, he supposed, other girls had just as pretty features.

But from the first time their teacher had asked them to work together on a project, his heart had been hers. "Hey, do you remember when we championed that auction for the Brown family?"

"How could I forget? What were we? Like twelve or thirteen?"

"We were twelve."

She shook her head. "We were far too young to be relied on to organize anything, let alone an auction for a family in need."

"We did it, though. We got volunteers and even asked Mr. Atle to be the auctioneer."

She tilted her head. "What made you think about that?"

"No reason." Only that he remembered a moment when they'd been feeling overwhelmed and underappreciated and had gotten a little slaphappy. They'd been in someone's barn, attempting to organize what had seemed like a thousand donated items when half of them had toppled to the ground in a heap. They'd gasped and stared at the mess. He'd uttered a few choice words under his breath.

But Elizabeth? She'd simply stood there and laughed—really laughed. It had been charming.

Elizabeth met his gaze now, and the tension between them rose. Then she hopped off her stool and waved a hand. "Randall, my grandmother told me what she said to you. I promise, there's no need to come here and grovel or beg."

"I think differently."

"You'd best get on with it then." She crossed her arms over her chest and obviously attempted to look mighty put upon.

"Elizabeth, I would like to apologize for my behavior yesterday."

"I accept it. *Danke.* So, um, are we done now?"

He winced. "Please don't be like this. I know your feelings are hurt, and I know I shouldn't have been so short-tempered with you yesterday. I really am sorry."

Her gaze softened as at last some of the reserve that had been so prevalent in her demeanor melted away. "Oh, Randall, I know."

"Danke." Some of the tension in his shoulders eased.

"However, if you don't mind me asking, why were you in such a snit? I mean, you had to have known that I was doing the best I could."

"I know you were." He'd also thought that her being there in the house had felt right. He'd wanted nothing more than to circle her in his arms and hold her close. Knowing that he'd had a chance to have her in his house as his wife, and had blown that chance to pieces, made his heart heavy. "And that, I think, is why I was having such a difficult time with you at the *haus.*"

"I don't understand."

"Elizabeth, I am just as aware as you are that we should have been married by now."

Right before his eyes, twin spots of color appeared on her

cheeks. "You are being presumptuous. You never asked, and I certainly never answered."

"That is true. But I think we both know that I was going to ask. And I, at least, felt sure what your answer was going to be."

Immediately, she averted her eyes, hiding her pain.

He felt that pain as clearly as if she'd thrust a knife in his heart. He pursed his lips, hating what he was admitting, but seeing no way out. "I broke things off because I felt my family needed me to be there for them. I thought it was my turn to be there for my siblings a hundred percent."

"Randall, everyone has responsibilities."

"I know that, but things are different for me." When she still looked skeptical, he said, "It is. We don't have anyone to lean on, to depend on."

"But if you truly cared, you could have leaned on me."

"That's not what I'm talking about. We don't have extended family here to give us guidance, Elizabeth. We don't even have parents." Thinking about how different and distant their father had been after their mother's death, he added quietly, "Actually, in a lot of ways, we've been raising ourselves for the last nine years."

He raised a hand so she wouldn't interrupt. "I know that for most of the time Junior bore the brunt of it. So did Beverly and Claire. But when each of them wanted to get married and have a chance to concentrate on their own lives for a change, I couldn't deny them that opportunity. I knew it was my turn."

"You are doing a *gut* job of it."

"Maybe, maybe not. All I knew at the time was that Junior had purposely not courted anyone seriously until Miriam, because he felt he had other responsibilities to the family. I was sure I needed to do the same thing. And that is what I am doing." Hating how weak and ineffective he sounded, he attempted to infuse his voice with a note of confidence. "This is the choice I've made, Beth. I need to stay the course."

Her brows rose, as did her voice. "You're acting like you ignored your responsibilities before Junior and your sisters got married. We both know that isn't the case."

"I did do a lot, but it was nothing like what Junior took on. The truth is, I was perfectly happy to let Junior do the hard stuff while I tried to be everyone's friend."

"There's nothing wrong with that."

"There was when I knew Levi was acting up, but I let Junior and Claire discipline him. There was when I was content to merely make money for the family, hand it to Junior, then go off to do what I wanted."

Lowering his voice, he added, "There was when I knew Kaylene was worried about school and I didn't offer to help her out because I knew Junior would help her . . . even if it meant he would have even less time for himself." Now that his pride was completely on the floor, he said, "Elizabeth, I'm struggling. I need help managing the house so I can concentrate on the finances and running the whole farm. I'm not asking for a second chance with you—I know I don't deserve that. But I can promise that if you do come back to work I'll do my best to be much more kind and appreciative."

"Because Kaylene needs me?"

"*Jah*. Because I think we all need you. It seems I've got quite a bit to work on. It's also obvious that I'm not going to be able to do it without your help."

As Elizabeth studied him, he realized how much he'd taken her for granted.

Elizabeth was pretty much perfect, and he'd been too shortsighted to try to keep her. He'd been so intent on being the man his brother was that he'd failed to look around and see everything he was in danger of losing. He hadn't taken the time to ask her to be patient with him.

"So, what do you say? Will you come back to work at our *haus*?"

"I say yes, Randall. I'll come back to work. I'll be there in an hour or so."

"Really?" Drat that hope that was eking out of his voice. He sounded so desperate. He *was* so desperate.

"Really," she said around a sigh. And then, thank goodness, she smiled. "I'm glad you came over to grovel. And I'm really glad we talked."

He was, too. He only wished that he had the courage to also tell her what was in his heart: that he'd made a mistake and he wanted her back.

He was too afraid, though.

He wouldn't have known what to do if she said that could never happen.

The moment Randall disappeared from sight, Elizabeth ran up the stairs.

"Lizzy?" her grandmother called out. "Lizzy, what happened?"

The polite thing to do would be to turn around and talk to her grandmother. But she just couldn't. She needed a moment.

Okay, she needed more than a moment to think about what had just happened.

When she got to her room, she closed the door behind her and closed her eyes. Randall had almost seemed flirty with her. Almost.

And she? She'd almost forgotten that he wanted her to cook and clean for him and his siblings.

After rapping on the door twice, her grandmother opened her door. "Elizabeth, what happened?"

"Randall said he was sorry, and so I'm going to go back over there in an hour."

"You don't fear that you're making a mistake?"

"Oh, I'm fairly sure going back over to the Beilers' is going to be a big mistake. But I'm still going to go."

"Care to explain yourself?"

"Not really."

Her grandmother leaned against the doorjamb, her arms folded across her chest. "Care to answer me again?"

"Mommi, the Beilers are paying me good money, and we can use it."

"No paycheck is worth your heartache."

"You're a dear, but I need to do this."

Worry creased her grandmother's brow. "I will write your mother today and explain to her that we still need her assistance."

"Please don't. It's not necessary."

"It is, child. I know the reason you aren't working somewhere full-time is so you can look after me." Her voice started to quiver. "Sometimes I can't even believe how much trouble I've become."

Oh, but it was hard to hear her grandmother speak like that, especially since she was the one person Elizabeth had always been able to count on. "Don't talk like that, Mommi."

"It's true."

"All that's happened is you've gotten older. Never are you trouble." She sighed, then admitted the truth. "I'm not going back only for the money. I'm going for personal reasons, too."

"Oh, I am sure that you are."

Elizabeth really hated when her grandmother was smug. "Randall's little sister is having a time of it, I'm afraid."

"That girl has a whole lot of siblings to look out for her."

"All right, fine. Mommi, even though it's going to be difficult, I need to return to their *haus* in order to face things with Randall," she at last admitted. At last admitted what she didn't even want to admit in her heart. "In spite of everything, I still have feelings for him."

Mommi sighed and straightened. "I was afraid of that."

"Why?"

"Because I have a feeling that Randall Beiler still has feelings for you, too."

Immediately, her cheeks burned. "It doesn't matter if he does or he doesn't. But we need to settle things between us. Become friends again. We can't simply go around avoiding each other for the rest of our lives."

"If that is why you are going back, then I think you should. As much as I'd like to always protect you from hurt, allowing yourself to confront fears is for the best. We can't move forward if we're always revisiting the past."

"*Danke*, Mommi. I needed to hear that." Feeling her eyes tear up, Elizabeth hugged her grandmother. "Now, I really better change clothes."

"All right. Um, Lizzie?"

She paused. "*Jah?*"

"Little girls like heart-shaped cookies. Take the cookie cutter and make some cookies with Kaylene."

Just thinking about all of Neil's laundry alone made her shake her head. "Maybe another day. Cutouts take a lot of time. . . ."

Her grandmother's tone turned firm. "Elizabeth, listen to

what I'm saying. That little girl needs heart cookies more than a clean bathroom. Make some cookies with her."

"All right, Mommi." There was no way she was going to argue with her grandmother when she used that tone of voice!

When Elizabeth was alone again, she pulled out her favorite raspberry-colored dress. After unpinning the dark blue one, she slipped on the fresh dress and began fastening it. For some unknown reason, she felt compelled to change dresses before going to the Beilers' house to cook and clean. It was vanity, for sure and for certain.

Definitely a mistake.

But she couldn't deny that looking fresh and pretty while in the Beiler house was important to her.

Five minutes later, Elizabeth had a blue sweater on over her raspberry-colored dress and had one heart-shaped cookie cutter in her hand.

"Lord, I hope you know what you're doing," she said as she started walking down her driveway. "Right at this minute, I feel like I'm Daniel entering the lion's den. Woefully unprepared."

chapter eleven

"Judith, I have to say that I haven't seen you so blue in months," her mother said when she bustled into the office at the back of their family's store. "Not since you had your miscarriage."

Judith inwardly winced. What was it about her *mamm*? Somehow she was able to bring up even the toughest, most heart-wrenching subjects without a qualm! Of course, she also had a special way about her. Somehow she was able to broach those tough subjects in such a way that would encourage Judith to talk instead of run out of the room.

"You're right, Mamm. I haven't been this blue since I lost the baby." After taking a quick peek at James, she leaned back in her father's favorite chair. She'd ostensibly come to the store hoping to help with inventory. Unfortunately, so far all she'd been able to do was stare into space and worry.

That was a shame, too, because they needed the extra hands. Ben was out front working with her father. They were doing a booming business in rocking chairs these days, so her father spent much of the time on the front porch with customers.

Pulling up an old stool, her mother asked, "Are you worried about losing James?"

"Oh, *jah*. Of course I'm upset about that. But Mamm, there's buckets of other things running through my mind, too. I keep wondering what James's life will be like if he does leave us. Do you think he will be happy?"

"I can't think of a reason why he wouldn't be. You and Ben aren't the only people wanting to adopt babies, you know."

Ouch! There again was another of her mother's matter-of-fact, homespun statements, hidden under the guise of careful concern. Judith had a feeling her mother was peppering their conversations with them on purpose. Probably to remind Judith that she wasn't the only person going through heartache. "I hear what you're saying. And I realize that I'm not the only person in the world going through such struggles. But . . . James, he's so young now. I bet if he gets taken away, he'll never even remember Ben and me."

The moment she finally said what was in her heart, the lump in her throat that she'd been trying so hard to will away returned with a vengeance.

Carefully setting down the Amish doll she was hand stitching—another of their top sellers—her mother considered her words. "Do you truly need James to remember living in your home?"

"I shouldn't, but I do." Glancing into the baby carrier again, where he was still soundly asleep, she said, "He's been important to me, Mamm. I know I'll never forget him. I know it's selfish, but I want to matter to him, too."

"You certainly matter to him now."

She mattered because she saw to his basic needs. But perhaps there was more to motherhood than merely taking care of bottles and diapers? "Is it wrong to want to matter to him for a lifetime?"

"*Nee*. But perhaps you are being a little too anxious about things you don't need to worry about just yet. Each of us makes a difference in other people's lives, Judith. Think of the stone that gets thrown into a quiet pond. Those ripples span out in all directions, remember?"

"I hear you, Mamm." Yes, she did hear her mother. Yet she couldn't help but be disappointed by all the folksy sayings she was hearing. She needed something more personal from her mother.

After giving her a long, meaningful look, her mother picked up her needle and thread. "What you are experiencing happens to everyone, Judith. It's a mother's lot to let her children go."

"Even for you?"

"Even for a mother of seven," she said with a sad smile. "It's hard to let them grow up and make their own decisions."

"I think it's hard because James is just a baby. He's not old enough to make these decisions. Someone is doing it for him."

"You're right, dear. It's different for you. And that will be hard. Terribly hard." She shrugged. "But letting him go is what might happen. You should prepare yourself."

"I thought you'd be more sympathetic, Mamm."

"I am sympathetic, but I also feel that I should remind you that all of what has been happening isn't your plan. You wouldn't have asked for a miscarriage, or fostering a prisoner's baby, or even facing the possibility that you may not be the adoption service's choice to be a child's mother."

"All of it has been beyond my control."

"Indeed, it has. But it's the Lord's plan and not yours. Ain't so?"

"*Jah.*"

"If you believe that, then you also need to understand that for some reason, the Lord decided that little James was destined to be born into a mighty confusing situation. Don't forget that James didn't ask for this, either. He is who we need to keep mindful of."

Watching her mother carefully stitch the doll's arm together, Judith nodded slowly. "You're right."

"And Kendra? That woman is certainly facing her share of hurts! His poor mother is having to come to terms with her choices but also with the fact that she might not live much longer. And imagine how it must hurt her to not even have the baby's father's love or support. She's been all alone."

"She does have a lot of burdens," Judith agreed, feeling even more inadequate. Why did it always take her mother to put everything into perspective? Why couldn't she have come to these realizations on her own? "Mamm, even thinking about someone not wanting to be involved in their child's life makes me angry!"

"I don't blame you for thinking that. James's father must be mighty selfish."

"During one of our visits, Kendra told Ben and me that James's *daed* might have shown an interest in him if there was a chance he could get some money!"

"My goodness!" Her mother looked just as shocked as Judith had felt.

"That makes me glad he is not in the picture."

"What that man might not realize is that raising *kinner* is not for the weak of heart or spirit," her mother said with a gentle smile. "Why, there have been times when an extra hundred dollars would have made raising you seven a bit easier."

Knowing her mother was half teasing, Judith said, "Why, Anson alone has to be worth two hundred dollars all on his own."

Chuckling, her mother nodded. "What that man should

do is talk to folks about raising boys. I fear some of us might tell him so many troublesome stories that he'd want to run for his freedom."

Ben entered just as her mother was finishing her quip. "Are you two back here complaining about men?"

"Not at all. Only about raising boys." Judith grinned, unable to resist teasing him. "Boys can be challenging, you know."

"Because girls are so easy," he said sarcastically. "I suppose you were a piece of cake at fifteen!"

Primly, Judith folded her hands on her lap. "Of course I was."

"Is that true, Irene?"

"She had her moments." After a pause, she continued with a twinkle in her eye. "Of course, even little Maggie does."

"No she doesn't."

Ben looked shocked, which made Judith start laughing in earnest. "You know Mamm only brought up sweet Maggie to tease you! Everyone in the family knows you think she has no faults."

"She doesn't. At least none that I've seen anyway." A smile was playing on his lips, too. But Judith wasn't sure if that meant anything. Ben really did adore five-year-old Maggie Graber—and the feeling was mutual. Maggie spent hours in his company.

At last she felt light of heart. "Thank you for the laugh, you two. It's been too long since I laughed like that."

Walking over, Ben pressed his hands on her shoulders and squeezed them gently. "We need to remember to tease and joke a bit from now on, Judith. It's going to be good medicine for whatever happens."

"I agree."

"Did you need something, Ben?"

"Oh, I came in to tell you that Bernie just stopped by. We have a meeting with Kendra this Friday."

And just like that, the light mood dissipated.

Everything was about to change, no matter what they wanted or how they acted. Change was inevitable.

She was at the Beilers' home to work. In order to get a paycheck. So she could help out Kaylene. And feed Levi something decent. No boy could live on beans, potatoes, and overcooked chicken forever.

Yes. She was working here for all those reasons.

Definitely not to be near Randall.

Elizabeth hoped if she sternly gave herself those reminders often enough she might actually believe them.

At the moment, at least, it certainly did feel as if she was in the house to cook and clean. No one else was around and she was mopping, her all-time least favorite household chore. Leaning down, she squeezed the vinegar-water mixture out of the rag mop, then returned to doing her best to remove what looked like months' worth of dirt and grime.

It seemed that no one in the Beiler household enjoyed mopping much, either, she thought more than a little bitterly. The floors were a mess.

She was almost finished when the front door burst open. Luckily, she was right there to block everyone's path. "Halt!"

The lot of them froze. "What's going on, Lizzie?" Levi asked.

"I'm mopping. Actually, I've been mopping and mopping . . . and then mopping some more! So much that I'm startin' to wonder if any of you even know how a mop works."

"That's not fair," Levi said.

"It feels fair to me. You've let this floor practically get the best of you." Feeling vaguely like a nagging mother, she said, "Which is why you boys must take off those shoes before you step one foot on this floor."

Micah's brows rose over the top of his eyeglasses. "Did you just call me a boy?"

"I did." Resting both hands on the top of the mop, she looked sternly at the three of them. "Do you have a problem with that?"

"Ah, not at all." With economical motions Micah bent down, pulled on his laces, and then stepped out of his boots. "May I come in now?" He held up a sock-clad foot. "My socks are clean, I promise."

"You may." She waved her hand to Neil and Levi, too. "All of you need to take off your boots and leave them outside if you insist on coming in."

"Seriously?" Levi asked.

"Of course I am serious. Why, look at this floor. Notice anything different about it?"

All three men gazed at it. "Um, it's wet?" Levi asked around a dimpled smile, just as cheeky as ever.

"Good job, Levi. It is wet, and by the looks of things, that is an unfamiliar occurrence. If you must come in, come in. Otherwise, I'd rather you wait until it dries and I get the rest of the floors clean."

"And how long will that be?"

"Not too long. I'm almost finished, but then it needs to dry completely." Since she also wanted to wipe down some of the worst corners, she shrugged. "It will only be an hour at the most."

"An hour?" When each of them looked crestfallen, Elizabeth found herself having to bite her lips so she didn't smile. "Is this a problem?"

"Kind of," Levi said. "I've got to go to the bathroom."

Now smiling was no longer an option. She giggled. "Walk carefully, Levi."

"*Danke*, Elizabeth," he murmured before racing up the stairs.

As the other two men stood in place, she sighed. "Do you two need to go to the bathroom, too?"

Neil shook his head. "*Nee*. But I'd still like to go to the kitchen."

"Me, too," Micah said. "And I need to change clothes."

Just then Elizabeth noticed that his pants were coated in mud—mud that could drip on her clean floor. "Micah, what in the world did you get into?"

His cheeks colored. "I don't think you want to know."

Neil grinned. "We got a new calf today. Micah helped deliver it."

Elizabeth gulped. "So those clothes are stained with . . . cow?"

Micah winked. "Yep. And I'm smelling kind of pungent. I need a shower in the worst way. Will you let me in now?"

If she knew him better, she would have made him take off those pants at the front door. But no doubt, that would be a bit shocking.

"Come on in," she grumbled. "Try not to touch anything when you go to your room."

"I'll do my best," he said almost meekly as he strode by her, leaving both a faint dusting of mud and grime and a definite cow scent in his wake.

"Come on in, too, Neil. How come you aren't dirty?"

"I've got a bit more experience," he said as he strode into the kitchen. "Plus, I made Micah do most of it."

"Ugh."

Neil shrugged. "We're brothers. We aim to make each other do things we don't want to do."

"It seems I have a lot to learn about being around so many people," she mumbled to herself as she hastily cleaned up the latest footprints. "Especially boys."

"Don't worry, Lizzie," Levi said as he trotted by her, now looking very relieved. "You'll get the hang of us Beilers in no time. Every one of us is a fair sight better than Randall, anyway."

"You think?" Spying one last dirty patch, she mopped it up, then rested on the end of the mop with a happy smile. She'd done it. The floor was mopped and clean.

"Oh, for sure. We are all easier to be around than him. At least, lately," Levi said with a wink, just as the front door opened again, bringing Randall and Kaylene inside like a burst of fresh air.

All over her clean floor.

"Your shoes!" Elizabeth cried.

"What?" Randall asked, standing there in the middle of the entryway, inspecting the bottom of each boot.

"Didn't you two see the pile of shoes outside?" Elizabeth demanded.

Kaylene peeked outside. "Now I do. Do you want our shoes off?"

"I surely do." She made sure to smile at Kaylene as she dutifully scampered out and pulled off her shoes. "And now you may go join your brothers in the kitchen."

Kaylene walked down the hall and was promptly handed a glass of milk by Neil.

Suddenly, she and Randall were alone again.

And just as if a flame had appeared between them, the tension in the air heated up.

Looking at her closely, he raised a brow. "What do you want me to do, Beth? Do you want me to take off my things as well?"

Her mouth went dry as she realized he had deliberately used her pet name and had purposely laced his words with innuendo.

Something had changed between them and he was flirting with her.

"*Jah*," she whispered. "I want you to."

"You sure?"

"*Jah*. When I am here, you must do what I say, you see."

After another long look, Randall turned, walked to the door, and pulled off his boots and his socks. Coming back in on bare feet, he stopped directly in front of her. "Now what do you want me to do?"

All sorts of bad ideas floated through her head. Things that had everything to do with memories of being in his arms and nothing to do with her mopping his floors.

Meeting his eyes, her mouth went dry.

Being around Randall this much was a mighty bad idea. A mighty bad idea indeed.

chapter twelve

Looking at Elizabeth, meeting her startled gaze, thinking about the way her lips were slightly parted, as if a pesky word that she just couldn't quite say was on the tip of her tongue, Randall knew that he was playing with fire.

He should not be teasing her, especially not in the suggestive way he was. It was too familiar, too sweet. It made them too close. Made him recall how much he was tempted by her. And made him remember just how much he'd lost when he'd broken up with her in such an abrupt way.

It wasn't fair, not for either of them.

"I know what I should do," he said with false brightness.

"You do?"

"I'll go dump this water out for you. Stay here and I'll be right back, okay?"

"But your shoes are off." She said that like it was a big deal. And made him realize that she, too, was just as affected by the sparks flying between them.

"I'll put them back on." Eager to put some space between the two of them, he practically ripped the mop out of her hands and took it and the bucket back out the front door. Two minutes later, his feet were in his boots and he was tromping to the side yard and dumping a bucketful of dirty water onto a patch of dry-looking grass.

He waited a moment, half expecting Micah or Neil to

come out and fill him in on how things were going. But after waiting for a few minutes, doing nothing more than watching the water seep into the ground, he went back to the front door, took off those boots, and padded into the kitchen.

The whole lot of them were sitting around the kitchen table, Kaylene next to Elizabeth. Glasses of milk and lemonade were out, and everyone was eating thick slices of what looked to be chocolate cake.

Randall's mouth watered. "You had time to make a cake, Elizabeth?"

"I did. Kaylene, I was going to make cookies with you this afternoon, but I was afraid we wouldn't have enough time for that. So I whipped up this box cake."

"It doesn't taste like a plain old box cake," Micah said.

"It's all in the frosting," she explained with a smile. "I found everything in your pantry and fridge to make a sour cream frosting, so I made that fresh. It makes a difference, I think."

Randall shook his head in wonder. He'd hardly been able to toss five potatoes in the oven to bake. Here in the span of less than three hours, Elizabeth was serving them thick slices of chocolate cake with homemade frosting—and apologizing for it! "I'm impressed."

Neil raised his brows. "That's all you have to say, *bruder*?"

"Well, I haven't tried it yet."

Looking gratified, Elizabeth stood and went to the cupboard for a knife and a plate. "Would you like a slice of cake, Randall?"

For some reason, he felt that if he gave in to the chocolate cake, he was going to give in to their attraction, too. And that was not why she was there. "I'll wait. It's close to supper time, you know." Feeling like a cad, he gripped that excuse like it was his lifeline. "Actually, all of you probably should have waited to eat your snack."

"I should have waited to eat my snack?" Neil murmured. "Who do you think you're talking to?"

"You know what I meant, Neil."

"I don't," Levi said around a disgruntled scowl. "Are you crazy, Randall? It's *gut*. Mighty *gut*. Plus, Elizabeth made a taco casserole for dinner. We'll eat that. You know we will."

"Perhaps." He glanced at Elizabeth. To his shame, some of the light that had been in her eyes had dimmed. He felt bad, but tried to tell himself that keeping things distant was better than the spark that had been between them when he'd first arrived. "But all the same, I'll wait."

Elizabeth put the knife down. "Of course."

In unison, his four siblings glared at him, making him feel like he'd just kicked a puppy.

After an awkward silence, Neil stood up and pulled out a chair. "You don't need to stand and wait on us, Elizabeth. Please, sit down again."

Her eyes darted from the empty chair to Randall and then back again. "*Danke*, but I'm all right. I will need to head home soon, anyhow."

"The cake, it is *wonderful-gut*, Elizabeth," Micah said, his voice sounding almost reverent. "Ain't so, Kay?"

"It's *wunderbaar*," Kaylene said with a sweet smile.

"Look at you!" Elizabeth said. "You have chocolate on your mouth." With an economical motion, she handed Kaylene a paper towel. "Wipe."

Kaylene wiped. "Do ya have to leave already?"

Elizabeth's expression softened. "I do, but I'll be back again tomorrow. Maybe then you and I can spend some time together, if you're not too busy?"

After Kaylene nodded, Elizabeth turned to Randall. "I'm going to head on home now."

"Wait. I'll walk you."

"There's no need. I'll be fine."

Knowing it would be best for the both of them to have their space, Randall nodded. "All right then. See you tomorrow."

Again, the three other men in the room gaped at him.

Finally, looking terribly irritated, Levi scooted his chair back with a screech. "How about I walk you halfway home, Elizabeth?"

"There's no need—"

"I'd like it. I need a break from the house."

Randall turned his back and pretended to be very busy going through the mail while Elizabeth told Neil how to heat up the casserole and gave Kaylene a little hug good-bye.

Only when the door closed behind them did he at last turn and breathe a sigh of relief. He was so mixed-up when it came to Elizabeth, he hardly knew what to do anymore. He hoped that eventually he could be around her without comparing their current relationship with their former one. Surely their time together would be easier to get through with practice.

"What was that all about?" Micah asked.

Turning around, Randall was surprised to see that their usually even-tempered brother looked irritated. "What?" he asked, though of course he knew.

"You know what. You couldn't have been ruder to Elizabeth."

"I wasn't rude. I just didn't want to eat any cake."

"You ran her off," Neil said as he gathered the dishes and started rinsing them. "She was just about to have a slice of cake with us."

"I didn't know that."

"You would if you hadn't been on some dessert patrol." Neil shook his head in disgust. "Since when did you care whether I'll eat my supper, anyway?"

Put that way, Randall supposed it had been a bit over the top. "Elizabeth was only supposed to be here for three hours. Her time was up. She's here to work, you know. It's a job." But of course, as soon as he said that he felt even worse. He knew she hadn't made that cake because she was getting paid to do it. No, it was obvious that she had been really trying to make them happy.

"Why don't you like Elizabeth no more?" Kaylene asked. "She's nice."

"What? Oh, I still like her."

"You don't act like it." Her eyes narrowed. "You know, I saw you kiss her once."

"You shouldn't have been spying on me, Kay."

"You shouldn't have been kissing her unless you were married."

As Neil sat by with a smug expression, Randall felt his neck heat. "There was nothing wrong with that kiss."

"Kisses," Micah corrected under his breath.

Kaylene frowned up at him. "How come you used to kiss her but now you only want her here to clean our *haus*?"

"The answer is complicated."

"It's not all that complicated," Micah corrected. "In fact, it seems pretty obvious to me."

"What is it?" Kay asked, her little foot tapping the floor. The very clean wooden floor.

"I don't owe you an answer, Kaylene. And you'd best stop using that tone with me."

"I wouldn't use it if you'd be nicer."

"Kay!"

"Kaylene, don't you fret," Micah said as he wrapped an arm around her shoulder. "Randall is just being a dummy."

"I'm not."

Kaylene rested her hands on her hips. "I don't know what's wrong with you, Randall, but I wish you'd go back to how you used to be."

And then, before he had a chance to chastise her, Kaylene ran up to her room.

Neil turned off the faucet. "Great job, Randall. That makes the fourth night in a row that our little sister has run up to her room."

"Hey—"

"I actually agree with her on this point. Things would be a lot better if you went back to how you used to be."

"That's not going to happen. Don't you realize that? We can't ever go back."

"I realize that you keep forgetting that you've got three brothers who are more than willing to help you."

"But you two have other things to worry about. I told you I'd take on the bulk of the responsibility now."

Micah raised a brow. "You said that, but for the life of me, I've never understood why. I'm smarter, and Neil is a better farmer. Listen, it's time you stopped trying to manage us all and start leaning a little bit."

"I know you are trying to measure up to Junior," Neil said quietly. "But don't forget that pride is a sin. Remember, even Junior leaned on Beverly and Claire. And the rest of us. He'd be the first to admit that, too."

While he was attempting to formulate a reply, Micah and Neil left the kitchen.

So he sat down at long last, wondering how he'd managed to single-handedly clear the room in less than thirty minutes.

That, at least, seemed to be something he could do well.

By the time she flipped the sign to Closed at the front of the restaurant, Pippa was so exhausted she was wondering how she was going to find the energy to walk the three blocks back to her apartment.

At the moment it felt like it might as well be three miles.

After making sure the front door was securely locked, Pippa strode back to her office to gather her belongings. But when she got to the soothing office and eyed the pair of comfortable swivel chairs that she'd recently put in the corner of the room, she felt an overwhelming urge to simply sit and put her feet up.

It had been one of those days. Everything that could have gone wrong had. Ruth—who never got sick—called in with the stomach flu. Then Jolene called in sick, too.

After that, things picked up steam. They ran out of split pea soup. And coconut cream pie. And meat loaf. Then some jerk from Cincinnati complained about the service and made Christina cry. And while she was crying, her brand-new husband, Aden Reese, came in.

And before Pippa could smooth everything out, Aden had informed her that he was taking his wife out for a break and that she'd be back when she was ready.

Which meant she suddenly became shorthanded again.

For the first time since she'd taken over the restaurant, Pippa was getting a pretty good idea about why her partner, Jana Kent, had longed for a break.

She spun her chair a bit, eyed the phone and her purse.

And then spied the canvas bag that Bud had left at her

place and that she'd brought to the restaurant to return, in case he ever stopped by again.

And then, of course, she spied the one thing she'd really been trying very hard not to look at—his phone number.

Maybe because she wanted to think of something besides the restaurant, she picked up the phone and gave him a call. If he didn't answer she would leave him a message.

Maybe even text him later.

He answered after one ring. "Hello?"

"Hi, ah, Bud," she stuttered, caught a bit off guard by how quickly he'd answered. "This is Pippa Reyes."

"Pippa?" His voice warmed. "It's good to hear from you. I wasn't sure if you were going to ever call."

"I wasn't sure if I ever would, if you want to know the truth." She took a deep breath. "The reason I'm calling is that I have your tote bag and your handkerchief."

"My what?"

"The handkerchief you loaned me the night you helped me with my groceries." When she'd teared up in front of him. "And your canvas tote."

"Oh. Well, I'd sure forgotten about those things. Neither is important; you can keep them."

"I don't think that would be right."

"Again, I haven't spared either a second thought. You should give them away or toss them in the trash if you don't want them."

Feeling strangely deflated—because now she had no reason to see him again—she made herself reply. "All right, then. Well, thanks, and I'll—"

"Wait. What are you doing now?"

"Oh, nothing much," she said around a tired sigh. "It's been a long day."

"You home?"

"Home? No, I'm not. I'm still at the restaurant but I'll leave pretty soon."

"Pippa, it's late," he said, his voice now sounding far more personal and less distant. "And it's dark out."

She peeked out her tiny office window. "I know that."

"How are you getting home?"

"The same way I always do. I'm going to walk."

"By yourself?"

"Yes."

"That's not safe."

"It's safe enough. It's how I get home every night, Bud. I'll be fine."

"You know what? I'm only five minutes away. How about I give you a lift?"

That curious combination of elation and apprehension raced through her yet again. "Oh, I don't know."

"Come on, Pippa. Take a chance. I'd like to give you a ride home . . . and maybe visit with you for a few minutes. What's wrong with that?"

"You know what? Not a thing. Thank you."

"Great. I'm on my way."

"I'll be waiting for you outside in the parking lot."

"Definitely not. I'll text you when I get there. Until then, you stay inside and put your feet up."

Taking off her shoes, she propped them on the corner of her desk. "My feet are now up," she said around a smile.

"Good. I'll see you soon."

He hung up before he said good-bye. And to her surprise, she kind of liked that. She actually liked not saying good-bye to him just yet.

She actually liked having something new to look forward to.

Getting to her feet, she decided to run a brush through
her hair and freshen up her lipstick. Not because she was
excited to see Bud or anything.

It just seemed like a good idea.

chapter thirteen

"He's so awful, Mommi," Elizabeth declared as she curled up on the couch late that night next to her grandmother. "I mean, really."

Just as she'd hoped, Mommi set her quilt square down and wrapped an arm around her shoulders. "What happened? And I'm assuming we are speaking of our friend Randall?"

Though Elizabeth heard the humor in her grandmother's voice, she was in no mood to joke. "Of course I'm talking about Randall."

"And what did he do now?"

"What *didn't* he do? First, he acted like he was glad I was there. He smiled in that slow, sweet way he used to. And even offered to pour out the dirty water from my mopping."

"Poured out dirty water, hmm? I suppose that is rather gallant. A perfect courting gesture."

She paused. "I know it doesn't sound romantic, but it kind of was."

Her grandmother's lips twitched. "I'll take your word for it."

"If you could have seen how he looked at me when he offered to help, you would know what I meant."

"That is *gut* then. *Jah?*"

"*Nee!*"

"Because?"

"Because just as soon as we joined the rest of the family he got distant. He didn't even want any cake."

Her grandmother clucked. "That does sound distressing."

This time Elizabeth couldn't stifle her giggle. "I made a chocolate cake, Mommi. His favorite."

"And why were you baking his favorite cake?"

"I don't know. No, yes I do. I wanted him to think about me." Even remembering all the flowery thoughts that had been floating through her brain while she'd been stirring cake batter was embarrassing. "Now, I don't know why I ever loved him."

"Oh, Lizzy."

"I'm sorry. I know I'm whining. But it's so hard. And he doesn't have to be rude to me."

"He was rude?"

"*Jah*. He practically ignored me."

"Well, it certainly sounds like he was in a bad mood. I wonder if he was sick? Sometimes men can be real bears when they're under the weather."

"Oh, Mommi. That's you, always thinking the best of everyone."

"I didn't know there was something wrong with that."

"There isn't. Not usually. But I can promise you this, Randall Beiler was not sick. He looked perfectly healthy when we first saw each other."

"Hmm. That sounds like a real puzzle, it does." With shaky hands, her grandmother picked up her chamomile tea and carefully sipped. After setting it back on the table, she murmured, "You said that Levi walked you part of the way home?"

"*Jah*."

"Well, what did he say about his brother? He don't seem the type of boy to keep his thoughts to himself."

"He's not. He said that he thought Randall was acting odd."

"And did he know of a reason?"

Elizabeth felt her cheeks burn and hoped that the dim light, combined with her grandmother's poor eyesight, would keep it from being too noticeable. "He suspected a reason."

"Don't keep me in suspense, dear. What does he think it might be?"

"Levi said that he thought that Randall still liked me."

"Ah." Her grandmother leaned back with a cryptic expression.

"Ah? Mommi, we both know that can't be right."

"And why is that? It sounds like a reasonable idea to me."

"When he used to come courting, he was different. He was kinder, more fun."

"Well, he does have quite a bit of responsibility now. Ain't so?"

"That's the thing. Why is he taking all of the family's problems on his shoulders? I know he really liked his construction job. When we broke up he had just been made a crew leader."

"Maybe he felt duty bound," she said as she slowly brought the cup back to her lips. "People do things that don't make a lot of sense, especially when they're thinking they're for all the right reasons."

That was a puzzling statement. Elizabeth pondered that, wondering if her grandmother was trying to tell her something without exactly telling it to her. She did that sometimes.

While she attempted to think of a way to ask her to explain herself, Elizabeth watched the journey of that cup filled with hot liquid up to her grandmother's lips.

As it wavered a mere two inches from her mouth, Elizabeth had to clench her hand so that she wouldn't reach out and steady it.

Of course she couldn't offer to hold the cup, but she lived in fear that one day her grandmother's shaky struggle was going to end with a spill of hot liquid all over her lap.

Perhaps the Lord was giving her a lesson in patience?

After she once again set the mug down, Mommi continued, just as if she hadn't taken a two-minute break. "You know, sometimes people take on things without thinking things through. Sometimes they imagine they are all alone, when in fact there are other options."

There she went again with her cryptic statements! "Mommi, won't you please speak more plainly?"

"I think I'm being mighty clear."

"Not really. What are you saying?" she asked impatiently. "Are you saying that Randall should have kept his job and asked for more help earlier rather than trying to sacrifice everything he loved to take care of his family?"

"That is not for me to say."

"But obviously you are hinting at something."

Her grandmother averted her eyes, seeming to suddenly be extremely interested in a piece of lint that lay on the sleeve of her dress. "Lizzy, what I am trying to say is that I see a great many similarities happening between you and Randall."

"Oh?"

"You both have chosen duty for others over yourselves."

"Randall cut back on his job because he has a large farm and siblings who are depending on him. I don't have that."

"You have me, though."

Elizabeth blinked. "Mommi, I like being with you. I like living with you. We are a team."

"We are a nice team. But my memory isn't so bad that I don't remember a time when I did a whole lot more work." She sighed. "Now I can hardly sip my tea without burning myself."

"I imagine that is hard."

"You are missing the point, Lizzy. I know I am now your burden. Whether you are bearing it joyfully or with remorse doesna make a great bit of difference." Leaning forward, she paused until Elizabeth was looking at her directly in the eye. "I am merely pointing this out so you will not be so hard on Randall. He has broad shoulders but maybe—just maybe—his burdens weigh heavy on him sometimes."

"I guess you are right."

Her grandmother burst out laughing. "You don't need to sound so grumpy about it, Lizzy."

"I'm not grumpy," she corrected. "Merely embarrassed."

"Embarrassed because I am right!"

Standing up, Elizabeth shook her head in mock dismay. "You're incorrigible, Mommi."

"I'm old and frail . . . but I'm still the same woman inside, Lizzy. As are you."

Elizabeth thought about those parting comments as she hugged her grandmother good night and walked down the hall to her bedroom.

Was she still the same woman inside, too? Under all the stress and worry and anger . . . was she still the same Elizabeth Nolt who had been in love with Randall Beiler?

Though he, Micah, and Neil had elected to not bother with

a large garden this year, Randall still found himself slipping on his soft, worn leather gloves, grabbing the old tiller, and preparing the soil for planting season.

Working on the garden gave him a link to his parents, and as he worked the soil as the sun rose over the fields, he allowed himself to remember them both. As always, it was a bittersweet exercise.

His memories of his mother were starting to grow faint. Oh, he remembered her blond hair always neatly arranged under her *kapp*. And the way she seemed to always know what all of them were doing at the same time.

But other things were starting to fade. He couldn't quite remember what her voice sounded like. Couldn't quite remember what she liked and what irritated her.

His memory of their *daed* was clearer, but more filled with pain and some anger, too, if he was being honest. Their *daed* had grieved so deeply for their mother that he'd become increasingly distant after her death. Sometimes Randall feared that their father had only considered his children to be a constant source of stress and worry. And reminder of the wife he had loved and lost.

They had all tried to give their *daed* time to grieve. Impatiently waited for him to snap out of his self-imposed isolation and begin to do more.

But that didn't really happen.

Months later, when it became apparent that their father wasn't going to be able to overcome his sense of loss, they'd all turned to Junior.

And Junior, at the too-young age of twenty, had borne their needs without a word of complaint. Before long, Randall was ashamed to remember that he'd simply assumed that his older brother would take care of things.

And Junior had. He'd slowly become head of the family, putting his needs last and the rest of theirs first. Doing his best to be both mother and father to little Kaylene. Even letting Levi sneak in his room at night when their little brother had bad dreams.

And now it was Randall's turn to keep things at the Beiler farm running smoothly.

Once Randall was satisfied that the rows were nicely tilled and the soil was prepped enough, he walked to the barn and got the bucket of onion, carrot, and potato seedlings he'd been holding on to.

Then he knelt down, pulled off his glove, and started digging into the soft earth with his fingertips.

"You always did like to play in the dirt," a voice said over his shoulder.

Randall looked up, grinning at his brother's appearance. Honestly, it was as if he'd just conjured him up. "Junior. Hiya. I didn't know you were coming by today."

When he made a move to get up, Junior waved him back down. "Don't get up. There's something about watching you plant that always makes me smile."

Smile? "I'm not going to ask why."

"Okay."

He couldn't help himself. "Okay, why?"

"Because you dig like Mamm used to. It didn't matter how many spades Daed bought her, she would disregard them and make perfect holes with her fingers."

"That must be where I got it from." He couldn't decide whether he was pleased to discover he had adopted one of their mother's traits—or embarrassed that he'd adopted a woman's habit.

After brushing off his hands on his pant legs, he eyed

his brother and said, "Any special reason you came by? You know, other than to watch me garden?"

"Yep. Miriam happened to see Kaylene this morning."

"Already?"

"She's helping out the new schoolteacher in the mornings," Junior explained. "Anyway, when she came home, Miriam told me that she was a little concerned about Kay. Said our little sister still seemed kind of blue."

"I've noticed that, too." Feeling even more ineffectual than ever, Randall forced himself to meet Junior's gaze. "Um, what did Miriam say Kaylene said?"

"First, Kay filled Miriam in about Elizabeth's chocolate cake and taco casserole. Said they were both great."

"Elizabeth is a *gut* cook, for sure."

"Then she told Miriam all about how grumpy you were."

"Junior, are you here because our nine-year-old sister tattled on me?"

"Of course not. But hearing about yesterday made me think that maybe you are feeling overwhelmed."

"I'm not doing any more than you did."

"I disagree. I had Beverly and Claire. They did all of the cooking and laundry. And they helped me look after Levi and the rest of you from time to time."

"Elizabeth is helping. And I am doing better. And as for Kay, it's true she is struggling a bit, but I seem to remember that the girls had their moments at that age."

Something appeared in Junior's eyes. Randall was afraid it was amusement. But maybe it was something softer? Something more like compassion? "Randall, I came over to tell you that Miriam and I talked about Kaylene again—about everything. We wanted you to know that we'd be happy to come back to live here."

"You can't do that. You just moved into your new house!"

"Miriam's folks can look after it day to day, and Miriam and I can visit there from time to time."

"That's a waste of a perfectly *gut haus*."

"It would be just for a while," he said slowly. "You know, until things settle down around here."

"Because it's obvious I'm not handling things well?" Guilt and disappointment with himself spiraled together in Randall's stomach. Everything that he had feared happening was taking place. It was becoming obvious to one and all that he was never going to fill his brother's shoes.

Junior shook his head. "I didn't say that. I'm offering because it wasn't fair to leave you with everything."

"You didn't."

"I pretty much have. Because I left, you had to practically quit your job and take up cooking. Now you're having to see Elizabeth often and having to deal with a grumpy Kaylene. It's too much."

"Hey. Kay is my sister, too. I want to be here for her. And I'm not alone. Levi has stepped up, and Micah and Neil are doing more than ever."

"I'm not saying everyone isn't doing their part. But it's still a lot for you to take on. Especially Kaylene. We both know she and I are pretty close."

A part of Randall was tempted. If he agreed, then he wouldn't have to deal with Elizabeth anymore. He could go back to his construction job full-time.

He could go back to being the way he was.

For some reason, however, he realized that he'd already changed. He liked knowing that he was currently responsible for their younger siblings. But was that selfish? Should he be only thinking of Kaylene?

"I'm not ready for you to move back."

"Are you sure? I won't think less of you."

"I know that. And I appreciate you saying that. But I'd like to give it a little longer before I throw in the towel. And let me talk to Kaylene, too."

"What about Elizabeth?"

"She and I will work things out. We're both adults, you know."

"Maybe the problem is that you two belong together."

"I used to think that. But now, I'm not so sure. I'm afraid too much has happened between us. I don't know how things will ever get better."

"All you have to do is take things one step at a time."

"You make things sound so easy."

"They are. I mean, they are if you let them be."

"Easy for you to say. You're happily married with a baby on the way."

"It's easy for me to say because Miriam and I had years to make up for. I practically ignored her for ten years straight. That's not easy to overcome, you know."

"I suppose it's not."

"Listen, it's easy to let past experiences rule your future. But if you really want to move forward, you need to start trying to make each time you two are together count. Don't simply dwell on the past. Stop and see if there might be a future."

He hated to admit it, but Randall was beginning to think his older brother made a lot of sense. *"Danke."*

He laughed at Randall's stingy tone. "No problem."

chapter fourteen

As Judith and Ben walked through the security checkpoints at the prison, Judith couldn't help but reflect on how different she felt about this visit compared to their first visit.

Now, while she wouldn't exactly call the guards friendly, they certainly didn't look as scary as they once had.

James seemed calmer with each visit, too. Whether it was because James noticed that she wasn't as nervous being around so much concrete and bars or whether he, too, was more accustomed to the routine, he also seemed to take the journey in stride.

After they got settled in the narrow waiting room before being let into the visiting area, Judith propped James on her lap and let him play with the ties of her *kapp*. These days pretty much everything went into his mouth. If it wasn't her *kapp*'s ties, it was his fist or a cold washcloth . . . or whatever he could easily grab!

"James is determined to get that tooth," she whispered to Ben with a smile.

Ben yawned. "I hope he gets it soon so we can finally get some sleep."

She smiled. Ever since their late-night conversation and the reminders her mother had given her about letting go, she'd been feeling a lot better about everything. No longer did the future sound so scary, because she was trying her best to take her husband's words to heart. "We'll get through it, Ben. As will James."

"I'm glad you're back, Judith," Ben said, his gaze warm. " I like this positive attitude of yours."

"Me, too," she said softly.

Ben was playing patty-cake with James when a guard opened the door. "Kendra is going to be meeting with you both in a different room today," she said.

"Oh?"

For once the guard dropped her usual reserve. "We thought holding James might perk her up some. She's been having a tough time of it."

Judith barely had time to share a worried look with Ben before they were led into a small room with four chairs and a table. Sitting in one of them was a frail-looking Kendra, and to say that she looked far different from the last time they'd seen her was something of an understatement.

Kendra darted a quick smile at them before gazing at James with a look of pure adoration. "Hi, baby," she said, standing and reaching her arms out.

James's eyes widened, then to Judith's surprise, he tucked his face into her shoulder.

Time seemed to stand still as it became apparent that James felt most secure with Judith and not his mom.

But instead of feeling pleased, the action brought forth a new wave of sadness for Judith. Yes, she loved this baby and she yearned to raise him as her own. But never had she wanted it to be at the expense of Kendra's pain.

"Come here, buddy," Ben murmured as he pulled James from her arms. "Let's see your *mamm*. I think she could use one of your hugs. Kendra, maybe you should sit down?"

"Yeah. Sure." Slowly, she walked to the table.

Though the baby didn't complain about going to Ben's arms, he turned his head so he could keep an eye on Judith. When Ben was about a foot away, James jutted out his bottom lip and reached out two chubby arms toward Judith.

Kendra visibly flinched.

And Judith laughed nervously. "You know how he gets, Kendra," Judith said as she attempted to laugh away the awkward moment. "He probably doesn't know what to think about this new room."

"Maybe so." Kendra bit her lip, but smiled when Ben placed the baby in her arms. After a bit of squirming, he settled into her arms at long last. After pressing her lips to his cheeks, she cuddled him closer and murmured something into his ear.

Ben returned to Judith's side. She knew that he was feeling the same way that she did. They could sit in this room for an hour and not say a word. Kendra needed every second with James that she could get.

After five minutes or so, Kendra shifted her attention to them. "Before you tell me about James, I think we'd better talk about things."

Judith nodded. "All right," she replied. "Whatever you want to talk about is *gut*."

"I guess Bernie told you about my health?"

Feeling slightly dizzy, Judith nodded again. "*Jah*. How are you feeling today?"

"As weak as a kitten." She grimaced. "Sometimes it seems like the treatment is making me sicker than the disease."

"I am sorry for that."

"I know you are," she whispered. "You are a very kind woman, Judith Knox." After a moment, she said, "Did you also hear that James's father has come out of the woodwork?"

"*Jah*. I mean, yes." Glad Ben was right by her side, Judith added, "What do you want to happen?"

"I don't want him to have custody of James. I met with my lawyer here and we filled out some paperwork." She swallowed. "And then there's my older sisters."

"Oh?"

"Yeah. Listen, Katherine and Emma are nice ladies. They, ah, are nothing like me. They are married and have jobs. Emma has kids of her own." After a pause, she added, "Until recently, they'd given up on me ever changing. Now, well, we're a little better but it's probably too late."

"I'm sorry, Kendra."

She impatiently shook her head. "This isn't about me. Um, I'm telling you this, because I heard that they now want to see me and see my baby. Now that I'm dying and all."

Judith's stomach dropped. She knew Kendra was sick, but she didn't know that things had gotten that bad . . . that Kendra felt that hopeless. "You mustn't talk that way, Kendra. We need to keep positive."

Kendra turned her head so she was focused on James. "You're real sweet, but I'm not just talking. I am dying; it's true. The treatments they're doing aren't doing much good— even the doctors are saying that I don't have much time left on this earth."

Ben leaned forward. "We are terribly sorry for you, Kendra. We'll pray for you."

"You know what? Thanks." As a tear fell from her eye, she squeezed her eyes shut and hugged James tight. He squirmed and started to cry. "Sorry, baby. I think I squeezed you too tight."

James responded by squirming again and looking at Judith in a pleading way.

Kendra frowned. "I guess he wants you now."

Judith pretended not to notice. "He'll be all right, Kendra."

"No. No, he wants you, which is good." She stood up and, after pressing her face into his neck for a second, handed him back to Ben. "It's better this way."

Judith felt frozen. She felt so sorry for Kendra and was at a loss for what to do. She wanted to comfort James but she couldn't bear to cause Kendra any more pain.

"Thanks for coming," Kendra said. "But I just can't do this." Before Judith had even stood up, Kendra was knocking on the door. "I'm done," she whispered as she waited for the guard.

Judith shook her head. "Wait, Kendra. Can't we spend a little more time together? We usually have at least thirty minutes, true?"

The door opened.

"I know you mean real well, and I do appreciate it. But I just can't be in here another minute." As tears rolled down her face, she shook her head slightly. "I just can't," she whispered, then turned and left.

As they stared after Kendra, James squirmed in Ben's arms. When she caught his eye, he smiled a wet, gummy grin and laughed.

Tears pricked her eyes. "Oh, James. Look at you."

Today was the first day James had actively reached for her, jas as if she were his mother. It was remarkable.

As she took the baby from her husband's arms and held him close, Judith realized that this was both one of the best and worst days in her life.

She was a glutton for punishment. There was no other

reason Elizabeth could think of to explain why she was back at the Beiler house.

With an increasing feeling of trepidation, she marched up to the stately front porch and knocked on the shiny black door. Almost immediately, Levi opened the door.

"You're back! Neil and I were thinking you might not come over today."

If Levi only knew how close she'd come to staying away! She was determined, however, to put her best foot forward. So she opted for teasing. "Why would you say that? Because you all are such a mess?"

"Because Randall can be such an idiot," he replied baldly. "I'm glad you didn't take him too seriously. None of us do, you know."

After Levi closed the door behind her, she rubbed her arms with her hands. The warmth of the house felt good after walking in the chilly morning air. "Randall wasn't so bad."

"Sure he was." Looking positively gleeful, he folded his arms across his chest. "Micah told him that, too."

"I can only imagine how Randall handled that."

Levi's mischievous smile turned into a wily grin. "He hated it. But that's all right."

"Oh?"

"Sometimes we've all got to hear things that we'd rather not."

"That's mighty perceptive of you."

"I'm growing up. Some might even say that I'm fairly grown-up for my years."

Last Elizabeth heard, Levi had been in the midst of his *rumspringa* and sneaking around a little too much. "Is some girl from the high school telling you that?"

"*Nee.* I'm not interested in English girls."

"Are you interested in someone special?"

"Maybe."

"Who?"

"I'll let you know in a couple of days." After putting his hat on, he handed her a neatly written note. "We weren't sure you'd come back, but we were hopeful. Neil and I went ahead and wrote everything out for ya."

She scanned the note. "Thank you."

"See you later."

Elizabeth walked to the window and watched Levi grab his bicycle and pedal down the driveway. Scanning his note, she saw that he was heading to his job at the construction site.

After studying the note again, she set the kettle to heat on the stove. She washed a few dishes while it was heating, then added a tea bag and took a seat at the table. A hot cup of tea was going to come in handy while she planned her day.

It looked like Micah was at the library studying, Neil had left early to go to an auction, and Randall had left hours earlier for his construction job. Kaylene was at school.

And Randall had left her a hundred dollars in the drawer by the refrigerator so she could do some grocery shopping. Oh, and could she please make another cake or perhaps even a pie?

Walking over to the drawer, she found an envelope with her name on it. Inside were five crisp twenty-dollar bills.

It wasn't an unheard of amount. After all, there were five people to feed, four of them grown men. But after scrimping and saving and watching every penny for the last two years, Elizabeth considered it a small fortune.

It took some effort, but she forced herself to only take stock of the Beilers' pantry and refrigerator and not imagine what she would buy for her kitchen if she had such a sum. Deciding to make a lasagna, broccoli, a layered salad, garlic bread, and two pies, she made a grocery list and mentally planned her day. After she cleaned the bathrooms, she would take their horse and buggy to the grocery, make her purchases, and then be home in time to work on the laundry.

She had made great progress and was in the middle of the baking aisle at the store when Levi ran up to her. He looked both flushed and flustered.

"Elizabeth, I'm so glad I found you."

"What's wrong? Is it my grandmother?" Right away, she started imagining all sorts of things that could be wrong. Had her grandmother fallen?

"It's Randall." After taking a moment to regain his composure, Levi said, "Elizabeth, I'm afraid there's been an accident."

And just like that, her heart stopped.

chapter fifteen

Hardly aware of what she was doing, Elizabeth reached out and grabbed hold of Levi's arm. "What happened? Where is he? Is he all right?"

"He's all right," he soothed in a way that made him seem far beyond his sixteen years.

"Sure?"

"I promise." Because they were garnering the attention of the other shoppers, Levi directed the cart to the back of the aisle.

She was about to jump out of her skin. "Levi, tell me about Randall. Now."

Levi took a deep breath and looked deeply into her eyes. "Randall is in the hospital getting checked out, but he's going to be okay. A couple of the men on the construction site took him right to the doctor as soon as he fell."

"Fell? Levi, what happened?"

"Randall was up on top of the house, helping to set some trusses like he always does, when he slipped and fell. It was the strangest thing, to be sure."

"I can't believe he fell." She winced as she pictured such a scene. Randall was always so sure of himself on the job. He had never had any kind of accident, which was why he had been promoted to crew leader. While accidents could happen to anyone, she was shocked to hear about him falling on the job.

"Me, neither, if you want to know the truth. Usually, Randall scampers around the shells like he's a squirrel in September."

"How badly is he hurt?"

"Last I heard, he's got some cuts and bruises, but his leg got the worst of it. They're pretty sure it's broken."

"Poor Randall."

"Yep." Levi shook his head. "Our foreman said accidents happen, and it's usually no one's fault. But it sure surprised me. I kinda figured he could do anything. Randall's always been fairly nimble. It's a real shock."

"Levi, you don't look shocked. You look mighty composed!"

He backed up a step. "We are in the store, you know."

"I know, but I can't believe you're so calm." She wanted to rush out to the street, flag down a passing car, and order it to run her to the hospital. "We need to get out of here."

Levi nodded and grabbed the handle of the cart and started pushing. "If you want to know the truth, none of us was all that calm at first, but Randall's been at the hospital for two hours now and the doctors and nurses don't seem to be overly concerned. They think he's going to be okay."

"He's already been there for two hours? Levi, his injuries must be really bad."

Awkwardly, he patted her on her back. "Elizabeth, I'm sorry to say this, but I kind of think you need to settle down a bit. Like I said, Randall's banged up and stuff, but he's going to be all right. Right now you're looking like you're about to faint or something."

"You promise it's not worse than you're saying?"

"I promise. We don't have anything to worry about. At least, not yet."

"Not yet?"

"Well, when I left to come find you, they were takin' x-rays to see if he's going to need surgery."

"Surgery?" Oh, but the news got worse and worse!

Just then she realized that so far Levi hadn't given her a word of explanation about why he'd tracked her down at the market. Surely if it was just to pass on the news about Randall's accident he could have waited until she got back to the house?

"Why did you come find me?" she asked. Hope filled her as she thought of what could be the only reason. "Has Randall been asking for me? Does he want me to come to the hospital to sit with him?"

"Oh, no." A line formed between his brows. "Well, I mean, I sure don't think so. I came for a different reason. Because Micah asked me to."

"Oh? What did Micah want you to do?"

He took a deep breath. "Elizabeth, we all hate to ask this of you, but could you stay over for a couple of nights?"

"Why would you need me at your *haus*?"

"If Randall does need surgery, we're all going to be wanting to be at the hospital. And if he comes home, well, it's obvious that we can hardly manage things when everything is going smoothly. I don't know how we'd manage it with this going on."

"I see."

"We're still kind of helpless, you see." When she didn't smile at his joke, he awkwardly continued. "And then there's Kaylene. She's still going to need to go to school and get her meals and such. I would ask Junior and Miriam to help with her, but they already have plans to go away for the weekend. We've all been trying to convince them not to cancel, especially since she has a baby on the way."

"I don't know, Levi. I mean, I have my grandmother. She can't see very well. And though she's spry, I can't let her stay home by herself."

He slumped. "Oh, of course not. I'll let Micah and Neil know. I'm sure we could figure something else out." Steeling his shoulders, he said, "Are you almost done with your shopping? If so, maybe I could ride back to the house with you. I ran over here from the hospital."

She knew what she could do. She could take Levi back to his house, fix them all a good supper, then walk home. What happened to Randall was a shame, but it wasn't her problem. And though they'd asked her to help with Kaylene, the truth was that Levi or Micah or Neil could probably manage just fine. It wasn't like she was a baby.

But even though all of that sounded correct . . . she knew in her heart that it wasn't what she should do.

And that was to be there for Levi and his family. And yes, for Randall, too. Even though he might not love her anymore, she knew she'd never forgive herself if she ignored his needs. That wasn't who she was, and it wasn't who she wanted to be.

"Levi, if it wouldn't be too much trouble, would you mind if my *mommi* came over to stay at your house, too?"

His eyes widened. "You changed your mind?"

She shrugged. "I suppose I did. The truth is that I would be happy to help you all, as long as I can look after my grandmother, too."

"Do you think she would come? You don't think she'd fuss about leaving your place?"

There was such hope in his eyes she almost laughed. "Actually, I think she'd enjoy it. She gets tired of sitting home by herself."

"That would be terrific." He brushed a stray chunk of hair away from his face. "Elizabeth, how about we go by your *haus* on our way back?"

"I think that sounds like a *gut* idea." Looking into the cart, she added hesitantly, "Do you think your brothers will mind if we eat your food, too?"

His brows raised. "I think they'd mind if you didn't eat with us. Come on, let's get your shopping done and pick up Miss Anna Mae. We're all going to have our hands full as soon as Randall gets home."

Elizabeth giggled. "Levi, sometimes I think the Lord made a mistake when he made you one of the youngest in your family. You have a true gift for organizing."

"I've thought that a time or two myself," he said around a grin.

With Levi's help, Elizabeth finished her shopping trip in record time. And, thanks to her careful planning, she only used a little more than sixty dollars.

Putting the change in an envelope, she said, "Would you like to keep this, Levi?"

"What are you talking about? That's your grocery money. Randall left it for you."

"But don't you think it would be better held by someone in your family? I don't want you to have to worry about what I'm doing with it."

"Don't talk like that, Elizabeth. You know we trust you," he said as they deposited the groceries in the small area behind the buggy's bench seat.

Then, after letting Levi take the reins, they hurried over to her house. To her pleasure, her grandmother agreed whole-heartedly to go to the Beilers' house.

Levi had volunteered to stay outside with the horse so

Elizabeth could talk to her grandmother in private. After she ran out and said that her grandmother would definitely be coming, she ran back inside and gathered some clothes, face soap, and her toothbrush as quickly as she could.

The moment she opened the front door, he rushed up the walkway to greet them. "Hiya, Miss Anna Mae. I'm glad you're coming over for a spell."

"I wouldn't miss it for the world."

They continued chatting the whole way back, Levi and her grandmother catching up like fast friends who had been apart for too long.

When they arrived at the Beiler farm, Beverly and Joe were there to greet them. "Elizabeth, it feels like old times, seeing you here," Beverly said.

"I'm glad I could help out," she said simply, not wanting to dwell on how things used to be.

After getting her grandmother settled inside, a hospital van drove up. She stood on the porch and barely stifled a gasp when she recognized Aden Reese as he opened the side door. Then she remembered that he worked in the hospital as an orderly. Competently, Aden helped Micah lift Randall out of the backseat.

Randall's left leg was in a temporary cast. There were bandages on his face and a particularly large one on his left palm. "My poor brother," Beverly whispered. "He looks even worse than I imagined."

"Didn't they think he should stay at the hospital a bit longer?"

Beverly nodded. "He's such a big guy, it surely would have been easier on his brothers. But you know Randall. Once they cleared him to leave, he wanted to get back home as soon as possible." Pointing to the cast, she added, "Especially since there's still a possibility that he might need surgery. They're waiting for the swelling to go down before they make a final decision."

It did look as if his brothers had their hands full as they attempted to guide Randall up the stairs. By the time they helped him hop up two steps, everyone looked exhausted.

She tried to stay out of the way while Beverly paid the driver and Joe gathered up what looked to be Randall's tool belt. As they helped him through the front door, Randall walked by where she was trying to hide and their eyes met. For an instant, his gaze softened, and she imagined that they exchanged a wealth of words that were better left unsaid.

Before she knew it, Neil had sidled up next to her. "Glad you're here, Elizabeth," Neil said as Aden, Joe, and Levi helped Randall into the house. "And did I hear right that Anna Mae came, too?"

"I didn't want her to be home alone. I hope you don't mind?" she asked as she tried to keep from staring at Randall. It wouldn't do for everyone in his family to see her gazing at him like she was. She knew right at this moment that she couldn't keep her heart out of her eyes.

"We don't mind. We're glad you're here. As you know, we need all the help we can get," he said as he glanced toward the procession as it made its way into the house. "Oops, I think I better go help. Randall is kind of listing to the left."

When she walked back inside, her grandmother smiled. "Soon, all the Beilers are going to wonder how they ever survived without you."

Elizabeth groaned. "Mommi, you never fail to put a positive spin on things."

"That's why we need each other, dear. You tend to overthink things. I promise, the Lord looks out for us. He always does."

"I know you're right." Looking at the door to the master bedroom—Randall's room— she said, "Mommi, I'm going to go see if Randall needs anything."

"You do that. I'm going to get started on these piecrusts."

"Are you sure you're not trying to do too much?" She couldn't forget that they were there for her to work, not her grandmother.

"My hands might not work too well, but I've been making crusts longer than you've been alive, dear. Go now."

"Wish me luck."

"I'll wish you the Lord's blessings," she said primly. "Just as I always do."

Her grandmother had caught her again. She'd said time and again that she didn't believe in luck or coincidence. Instead, she was sure that everything came from the Lord.

So she closed her eyes and prayed for strength, and for the Lord's will to be done. But as she thought about how topsy-turvy everything was with Randall, she quietly asked for a little bit of luck, too.

At this point, she was going to take anything she could get!

chapter sixteen

Unable to wait another second to see Randall, Elizabeth hurried down the hall to his room. When it was obvious that his room was already full to bursting with his siblings, she paused, thinking to give them a moment or two of privacy.

Actually, she was about to turn around when she heard Beverly repeating the doctor's instructions about the medicine he prescribed, and Neil ordering Levi about. Thinking that was pretty important to hear, she stepped a little closer. If she heard the instructions now she wouldn't need to pester any of them about what to do later on.

"So you do understand that you are to stay in this bed unless you have to go to the bathroom?" Beverly said sternly.

While the others chuckled, Randall barked an answer. "I understand that I don't appreciate my sister talking to me about using the toilet."

"Watch it, *bruder*. I am your older sister. I'm supposed to boss you around."

"You've gotten pretty good at it, too."

"That's because I've had years of practice."

"Which means I should probably be glad that Junior and Claire aren't here."

"They would agree with me. Now, do you need to go?"

"*Nee*. I do not."

Elizabeth grinned. Even from her spot in the hall, she could hear the mixture of embarrassment and aggravation in Randall's voice.

"If you do—" Beverly began.

"If I do, I will definitely let someone know," he interrupted. "Not you, though."

Elizabeth had just stifled a giggle when Neil wandered out. Catching her eye, he grinned. "It looks like you caught most of that conversation."

"I was going to come in when I heard everyone talking, and thought it was pretty crowded in there. I was going to go back downstairs and give you some space, but then when I heard Beverly giving directions, I decided to listen in. I didn't know the conversation would turn so personal, though."

"He's a bit out of it. I hope our plain speaking ain't embarrassing you too much?"

"Not too much," she said with a smile.

Neil grimaced. "He's acting mighty loopy. We're all about to let him sleep, so you can go on in if you want, but I wouldn't stay too long."

She was about to say she understood when Randall's voice floated out the door.

"Neil, are you talking to Elizabeth out there?"

Just as she was about to call out that it was, indeed, her, Neil replied. "It is."

"But why does it have to be her?"

"Because she's willing to put up with you."

"But I don't want her here. Couldn't you have found someone else to play nursemaid?" Randall continued.

Next to her, Neil flushed. "You know what? I think you should visit him later. Much later. Let's go downstairs."

Elizabeth shook her head. "I don't think so."

"She's not playing nurse," Levi protested, his voice full of belligerence. "And you shouldn't be talking about her like that. You know she's been doing her best to help us."

"I may be stuck in a cast, but I can still talk to you how I like, Levi. You shouldn't have asked her to come over."

"I'm getting out of here," Levi declared, pure irritation thick in his voice. "I'm fair worn out. I had to run all over town when you fell. Not that you even care."

"No one told you to do that."

"Micah, get him to shut up, wouldja?" Levi said over his shoulder as he walked through the threshold. "I'm about to stuff a sock in his mouth."

When he spied her, Levi came to an abrupt stop in front of her. "Elizabeth, how long have you been standing here?"

"Only long enough to hear that I'm not wanted," Elizabeth murmured.

"You really need to ignore Randall. I promise that I want you here. We all do." With a glare at the door, Neil added, "Randall's going to drive us crazy within twenty-four hours."

"It won't take me near that long to be sick of him," Levi said.

Looking from one brother to the other, she felt a true mixture of amusement and confusion. "You two certainly don't need to be apologizing for anything he says."

"I don't want him hurting your feelings, though," Levi said.

"I'm tougher than I look," she countered. "I don't get my feelings hurt easily. Besides, I do want to know what he's thinking."

Both brothers were prevented from replying as Randall spoke again, his voice now even louder and more belligerent.

"Micah, can't you try to get her to leave? You know I don't want to be around Elizabeth any more than I have to."

Elizabeth supposed a better woman might have started walking down the hall. Would take pity on Levi's and Neil's obvious embarrassment. Perhaps even started talking about something else in order to pretend that she hadn't heard a single hurtful word.

But it was like she was witnessing a train wreck. She couldn't seem to do anything other than stand there like a fool and eavesdrop.

When Beverly rushed out of Randall's room in an obvious huff, she drew up short like her brothers and moaned. "Did you just hear everything?"

"She did," Neil said.

Now realizing that her standing there was only making things worse, Elizabeth pushed past Beverly and stepped into Randall's room. It was time to confront the grumpiest, rudest patient ever.

The moment she crossed the threshold, Micah and Randall looked her way.

"Hi," she said. After smiling briefly at Micah and noting that he looked just as aggravated as the rest of his siblings, she made a shooing motion with her hands. "How about you go take a break?"

Rubbing his back a little, Micah nodded. "You know what? I'm going to take you up on that. And please, try not to listen to a word he's saying right now. He's not himself."

"It's nothing for you to worry about." Looking at Randall, she decided right then and there she'd never seen him look worse. When they were courting, he'd always taken time to look his best.

Now he was a cranky mess of scrapes, bruises, and cast.

"So, I gather that you don't want me here? That you would like to spend as little time as possible with me?"

He grimaced. "I didn't mean what I said exactly the way you heard it."

"Oh?"

"Yeah." He groaned as he shifted on his pile of propped-up pillows. "I'm sorry, Beth, but I'm not doing too good right now."

Hearing him call her Beth, especially when it was obvious that it had just slipped out, made much of her irritation float away. Softening her voice, she murmured, "I kind of noticed."

"Listen, when I said I didn't want you here, it wasn't because I didn't want to see you."

"Why don't you want me here?"

"Because I don't want you to see me like this."

He looked so dejected that a bit of her hurt feelings started to dissipate. Actually, she was starting to get a very good feeling that there had been more to his words than she'd first thought.

"Are you in a lot of pain?"

"*Jah.*" He squirmed again. "And I canna get comfortable."

She fluffed the pillows behind him. "Here, try lying back again."

He shifted, groaned, then shifted again. After a couple of seconds, some of the tension in his face eased. "That's better."

"*Gut.*"

"Hey, Beth?"

"What?"

"Now that you're here and all . . . would you stay with me for a little while?"

Not bothering to tease him about his change of heart, she

nodded. Sitting on the side of his bed, she ran a hand gently through his hair. "*Jah*. I can do that."

"*Danke*."

They sat in silence for a while. Unable to stop touching him, she continued to brush that one stubborn lock of hair that looked in need of a trim.

When she saw him attempting to swallow a yawn, she said, "I think you should try to get some rest. Close your eyes."

Miraculously, he did as she asked. "So tired, Bethy."

"I know, Randall. Stop worrying and just rest. I promise, everything's all right."

As he shifted, then slowly relaxed, she ran her hand through his hair again.

Moments later, he was fast asleep.

To her bemusement, she was smiling as she walked back down to the kitchen. Her grandmother was there rolling piecrust—and, it seemed, offering a bit of comfort to the other Beiler kids. When Elizabeth entered, she smiled sweetly. "There you are, Lizzie. I was wondering when you were going to leave Randall's side."

"I wanted to wait until he fell asleep."

Levi looked surprised. "You got him to sleep?"

"Yep. He just needed to relax. I have a feeling he'll sleep for a couple of hours now."

Beverly, Micah, and Neil were sitting at the table holding mugs of hot chocolate. Levi was sitting on one of the countertops eating an apple and watching her grandmother.

Elizabeth met Levi's irritated gaze, Micah's sheepish one, and Beverly's pleading eyes. "Everyone, stop looking so worried. I am fine."

"Are you sure? I canna even believe that Randall was so rude," Neil said. "I've never known him to act like that."

"He is in pain, I'm afraid. I would be a terrible person if I held everything he said against him right now."

"Not terrible. Maybe justified," Beverly said darkly. "My Joe would never speak to anyone like that," she added as Joe walked into the kitchen through the back door.

After bestowing a fond look his bride's way, Joe said, "Do I want to know what she's talking about?"

"Nope," Levi said quickly. "It has to do with my fool *bruder*."

Joe's brows rose. "What has Randall done now?"

"It's really nothing," Elizabeth said as she filled the kettle with water and set it on the burner.

"It really would be best if you don't listen to him over the next couple of days, Elizabeth," Neil said. "Randall is chock-full of pain relievers. He doesn't know what he's sayin'. Actually, he probably won't even remember."

As she went to make herself some tea, she figured Neil was right. Randall couldn't be held responsible for the things he was saying. There really was a very good chance that he wouldn't remember a single thing he said.

Now all she had to do was figure out a way to forget everything he said, too.

chapter seventeen

"So, I can't wait another minute before I ask," Christina declared as she delivered a stack of freshly cleaned menus to Pippa. "Who's going to pick you up tonight, Pippa?"

The question caught her off guard. "Is it that time already?" she teased.

"Already?" Christina rubbed the back of her neck. "The time has gone by quickly, but not that quickly! I started thinking about taking a hot bath about two hours ago."

"A hot bath does sound like heaven. Anything to soak my feet."

"Definitely my feet. And my arms! I'm going to be so sore. We sure had some big tables."

"We did. It was a good night."

It had been an unusually busy night of service. Much to her surprise, her Mexican dishes were slowly gaining a steady and very loyal following. Two weeks ago she'd instituted Mexican-food Mondays, offering three Mexican-themed specials. Word had soon gotten around, and tonight they'd run out of both the vegetarian chalupas and the chicken enchiladas.

All she'd been doing for the last hour was counting down the minutes until she was able to sit down and put her feet up.

And that was probably the reason she did a double take when Christina asked her question. "I'm not following you."

"Sure you are. The last two times you've gotten a ride, it was that handsome man picking you up. The girls in the back and I want to know if he's going to return anytime soon."

"That man would be Bud."

"Bud." Christina rolled his name on her tongue. "That's a short and sweet name."

"I think it's short for Robert."

Christina wrinkled her nose. "Really? I like Bud better than Robert. I think Bud's got a real nice ring to it."

Pippa chuckled. "You are silly. But you might be right about that. I like his name, too."

"So . . . is he going to pick you up today?"

"I think so." She was becoming amused—in spite of the fact that she could practically feel her neck and cheeks turning an embarrassed pink. "Now, do you care to tell me why you are all so interested?"

"Why do you think? He's mighty handsome."

"You're embarrassing me."

"I'm sorry. But, you shouldn't be embarrassed. You don't have anything to do with his looks."

"I suppose you're right about that." Bud had broad shoulders, hazel eyes, and a square jaw. In her more fanciful moments, she liked to think he looked a lot like one of those movie stars of old.

"It's exciting that you are going courting."

"You . . . you think so?" She wasn't all that sure what "going courting" actually meant. But she knew it was what the Amish folks around here did instead of dating. Despite being still a relative newcomer, after getting to know so many of the Amish women working at the inn, she was starting to understand their customs.

"To be sure! Why, all of us have been having a grand time

watching you wait for your admirer to take you home. It's mighty romantic."

She was embarrassed to let Christina realize how much she hoped that she actually did have an admirer—and not someone who was just feeling sorry for her. For someone who felt so at home running a busy restaurant, she was certainly feeling insecure about her love life. "Christina, do you think maybe Bud is only stopping by and taking me home because he feels sorry for me?"

"Why would he feel sorry for you?"

Now she had done it. Ever since she'd started at the Sugarcreek Inn, she'd tried to remain professional and detached. Jana had said that by keeping a little distance it was easier for her to give the other girls directions. But Pippa was by nature a social person. It was difficult for her to not want to be friends with the other women whom she worked with. "No reason."

"Come on and tell me." She leaned forward. "Do you and he have a secret past?"

"What an imagination you have! Nothing like that. It's just that, well . . . Bud and my ex-husband are friends. Sometimes I feel like he knows that I am a little lonely these days."

Christina raised her brows. "Is it awkward, knowing that Bud and your ex talk to each other?"

"It is. But I'm also learning that Bud didn't necessarily agree with how my ex-husband treated me." Realizing that she couldn't leave it at that, Pippa added, "Miguel and I got married very young. We grew apart and started fighting a lot."

Unfortunately, that had been the least of it.

Christina's light blue eyes turned serious. "I'm sorry to hear that, Pippa."

"No reason to apologize. It's water under the bridge."

"Is it? Well, from what the other girls and I can tell, Bud seems to treat you good."

Pippa smiled, enjoying the way that Christina referred to all the girls being interested in her. "He does. So far, he couldn't have been kinder." Sometimes he said the sweetest things, and made her feel almost pretty, too.

She opened her mouth to add what else she was thinking, but shut it just as quickly. It was wrong to share such private thoughts about someone who had done so much for her.

After seeing that none of the four tables that were filled seemed to need anything, Pippa took a plunge. "How are you doing? Is married life agreeing with you?"

"Oh, *jah*," Christina replied with a dreamy smile. "Being married to Aden is everything I dreamed it would be. *Wunderbaar.*"

"You, my dear, are a smitten newlywed."

She blushed. "I can't help it! When Aden lost his parents ten years ago, he moved in with us. Sometimes I feel like I've spent most of my life waiting for our friendship to bloom into something stronger." Before Pippa could comment on that, Christina rushed on in a darling, giddy way. "You know, my *mamm* says we make her feel old. But she also whispered that she thinks all newly married couples should be so in love." She sighed. "It's nice, you know?"

So in love. Pippa couldn't remember if she and Miguel had ever considered themselves that way.

Which was a problem.

"It sounds very nice. And you have your own place, too." Thinking about the history of Christina and Aden's apartment, and how it was a little off the main strip, she asked, "Is it strange, living above the old hardware store?"

"I thought it might be scary, but I kind of like it. Aden works at the hospital in Millersberg, you know, so he has to take a van to get back and forth. He used to have to go to the livery, hitch up his horse and buggy to get there. Now, because we live so close, I can walk right here and Aden can walk to the van. Plus, we both agreed that we needed some time to ourselves. My parents offered to expand Aden's room into a little apartment, but neither Aden nor I wanted that."

"I wouldn't have wanted that, either." Pippa was genuinely happy for her sweet, young employee. Of course, there was a part of her that wished she could be that carefree. Sometimes she felt like she was double her age, carrying around her baggage from her first marriage. "It sounds like you and Aden are off to a good start. I couldn't be happier for you. And I'm very thankful that you're still working."

"I like working. Aden and I aren't quite ready to start our family. So if I didn't work, I'd be at home alone all day. This is a *gut* job for me. And I really do like waiting tables."

"If things change, please talk to me before you do something drastic and quit."

She smiled. "I promise that I will do that. Pippa. Me and the girls really like having you as our new boss."

"You do? Thank you for telling me. I know it's been hard, trying to get used to a new manager."

"You've been easy." She fiddled with her apron, then blurted, "And if you don't mind me saying so, I hope you give Bud a chance."

"I will, if he still wants to give me a chance. I'm a little out of practice when it comes to dating, you know."

"You must be doing something right, because he always looks at you like he can't look away."

"Now you're really making me embarrassed." She would

have said more but she spied Bud walking down the sidewalk. "Oh! Here he comes."

She'd just walked to the door when her heart just about stopped. Bud wasn't alone today. He was with Miguel, and they were both talking animatedly outside the restaurant.

Her heart sank. Had Bud only been pretending to get to know her so he could report back to Miguel?

"I need to go talk to Bud outside. Look after the last tables of diners, would you? I think they're almost done." She walked out without bothering to hear Christina's reply.

Both men were still in deep conversation when she walked out to join them.

She was so fired up, she didn't know who to talk to first. She decided they both needed a piece of her mind. "What's going on? Bud, why are you here with Miguel?"

"That's a fine way to greet me—" Miguel began.

"We're divorced. I don't have to greet you anymore. Why are you here?"

"Can't we talk about this inside?"

"Definitely not!" And have everyone in the restaurant, including all her employees, overhear her conversation? That was the last thing she needed!

Bud glared at Miguel. "This was exactly what you promised not to do." Then, turning to Pippa, he said, "Pippa, Miguel stopped me on my way over here. He found out we've been dating."

"And?"

"And what do you think?" Miguel asked. "I don't want you two seeing each other."

Bud raised a hand before she told Miguel exactly what she thought about that. "I don't want to fight. Since I had promised to pick you up, I thought maybe we could talk about things for a few minutes."

"And then what? We'll all drive back to the complex together?"

"He brought his own car." After giving Miguel another warning glance, Bud said, "Please, Pippa? Can we talk things out? I really do think it's better to have everything out in the open."

She wasn't so sure she agreed, but she realized that she didn't have much choice. Whether she wanted to have this conversation or not, it was about to happen.

With a sigh, she pushed open the door. "Well, let's go get this over with."

And after they talked, she had a very good feeling that she'd be walking home.

Obviously, dating her ex-husband's friend hadn't been a good idea, after all.

The first thing Randall noticed when he opened his eyes was that every bit of him hurt. He kind of felt like he'd been run over by a Mack truck, and then the truck had reversed and taken another swipe at him.

The second thing he noticed was that Elizabeth Nolt was sitting by his side.

"Hey," he mumbled. "You're here."

"And, you're up. At last." She smiled, but there was a new, guarded look in her eyes.

That worried him, but he was too bleary to remark on it. Plus, it felt as if his mouth had been stuffed with cotton. He awkwardly tried to clear his throat. "Have I been asleep for long?" he asked, then frowned as he realized he sounded like he'd swallowed a frog.

"Awhile. Four hours, give or take." Her voice warmed. "You've slept long enough to be ready for some pain reliever, I think. And maybe something to drink, too?"

"That sounds real *gut*. Danke."

"I'll be right back."

He nodded, then immediately regretted the motion. His head was pounding.

She rushed out, then returned moments later with Neil by her side. "Look who I found."

Her voice sounded unnaturally cheery. "Hey," he said. Though he appreciated his brother taking the time to check on him, Randall was suddenly eager to spend some time alone with Elizabeth. If his head ever cleared, he hoped to discover what had put the new line of worry on her face. Unless she was just concerned about his injuries?

After handing him a glass of water, Neil pulled up a second chair. "Glad you could join us again. We were starting to worry."

"What happened?" he asked after he nearly drained the glass.

With a frown, Elizabeth pulled the glass away from him. "Careful, you're supposed to sip."

While Elizabeth left the room, presumably to get him more water, Randall turned to his brother. "Neil, the last thing I remember is balancing on a joist."

"That's probably because right after that you slipped and fell almost fifteen feet. As soon as you fell, your supervisor called nine-one-one and they rushed you to the hospital. Another person on your crew took Levi around to tell us the news."

"Wow."

"We were all real worried. You were unconscious for a few minutes, long enough to give us all a scare."

"Wow. I had no idea."

"It's a wonder you weren't more badly hurt," Neil said. "But then, just as we were all sure we were going to be camped out at the hospital for the next few days, the doctors said you were complaining and doing better. I mean, better, considering that you've got a broken leg."

Randall glanced at the cast around his leg. "It hurts something awful."

"Lucky for you, I have your medicine," Elizabeth said, coming back into the room. "Open."

Feeling far too old for this, he did as she bid. She popped two pills in his mouth, then helped him take a couple of sips of water through a straw. When she leaned closer and slid a cool hand behind his shoulders it was all he could do not to moan in appreciation.

For a split second, it seemed like it was just like old times. They were a couple again, and when the two of them shared a smile, it felt like the rest of the world was suspended. That nothing mattered besides those few minutes when they were together.

As he gazed at her, her own expression softened, giving him hope. Until he remembered that they were in two different places now.

Deliberately, he turned away and pretended he was very interested in his cast. "Do they not use plaster casts anymore?"

"They don't give you permanent casts until your swelling goes down," Neil said. "We'll take you to the doctor in a couple of days to see how you fare."

"And that means you're going to have to be careful and let us help you," Elizabeth cautioned.

"I'm going to be stuck here in bed for a while, aren't I?"

"Yep," Neil said.

He hated the idea of being so dependent for days and days. "I don't know how I'm going to survive that."

Neil didn't look all that concerned. "You're simply going to have to. You don't have any choice."

"That's true."

"It is. And if you didn't try to fight us so much, you might find it easier than you think."

"I would, if I thought I really needed all this rest."

"You do."

"You've got a whole host of cuts and scrapes, too," Elizabeth interjected. "Randall, you needed stitches on your arm."

Feeling vaguely foolish, Randall lifted his arm and raised his brows at the bandage. "I don't remember getting those."

"It's no wonder. You're covered with bruises," Neil said. "It really is a wonder you aren't in the hospital right now. The Lord must have heard our prayers."

"Indeed. And your guardian angel must be working overtime, too. There's no other explanation."

"Although, you are a stubborn man, to be sure," Neil said with a grin.

"Stubborn and obstinate," Elizabeth agreed.

"I think those are the same thing," Randall murmured, realizing even this small interaction was tiring him. Already, his eyelids were getting heavy. "I don't know what's wrong with me, but I'm tired again."

Neil stood up. "That's my cue to get out of here. Get some sleep, *bruder.*"

When it looked as if Elizabeth was about to follow, he held out a hand. "Stay for a little longer, wouldja, Beth?"

After a second, she slipped her hand in his and squeezed

gently. "Just for a bit. You need to rest, Randall. The doctors said that sleeping is the best thing for you."

Her voice was so soothing. And now that she was back by his side, he could smell the honey-scented lotion she always used. It warmed his senses, making him feel like maybe he hadn't ruined everything between them.

But then he remembered their conversation in the kitchen and how rude he'd been.

And how he'd been sure that she'd never want to have anything to do with him ever again.

"Why are you really here?" he blurted, too groggy to put things more eloquently.

"Because I was asked to help tend to you," she replied.

Too late he realized that it would have been far better if he'd simply kept his mouth shut. He closed his eyes and wondered what it was about her that always brought out the worst in him. "Sorry. I didn't mean it like that."

"There's nothing to apologize for."

"I kind of remember saying something I shouldn't have. Did I?"

"I'm not sure. I don't know what you truly meant and what you didn't. The pain medicine had you kind of out of sorts."

He was feeling groggier than ever, but he was pretty sure he knew enough to regret hurting her feelings. "Beth, if I said something to hurt your feelings, I truly am sorry."

She sighed. "We are in a bad place, you and me. You are hurt."

"I'm hurt, but that's not all that's going on."

"I agree. You are trying to take care of your family. I am, too, I think." She frowned. "And sometimes when we try to take care of our families, we say and do things we wish we hadn't."

"What have you had to do or say that you regret?"

"I've let my pride interfere with my responsibilities. I should have contacted my *mamm* by now and told her that I needed more money. But instead of doing that, I've been scrimping and saving. And maybe worrying my grandmother too much."

"What happened with your *mamm*? Did she forget that you had bills to pay?"

"I don't think so. Maybe it's more a matter of me and Mommi being out of sight and out of mind. She's got a new family, now."

"I wish you didn't have to make things better by working here."

"You really don't want me here?"

That couldn't be further from the truth. The problem was that he wanted her too much. But he wanted her there on her terms. Mainly, he wanted her to want to be around him, not because she needed a paycheck. "That's not what I meant." Though his head was starting to hurt worse, he added, "Beth, it just seems to me that you could use some choices."

"I don't mind being here," she murmured.

"Sure?"

"I'm sure," she said quietly. "At least for now."

chapter eighteen

Because she was bothered too much by the conversation that had just taken place, the moment Randall started breathing evenly, she made her way down to the kitchen. She was determined to cook away her frustration and troubles.

If she was going to be steamed about the things that Randall continued to say to her, at least she could be steaming something in the kitchen.

She was pleasantly surprised that no one was in the kitchen. Before he'd drifted off to sleep, almost everyone had peeked in at Randall to make sure he was doing all right. She had imagined they'd be congregated around the kitchen table for the rest of the afternoon.

After opening the refrigerator and again feeling grateful that someone had put away the few groceries she'd managed to buy, she pulled out a chicken, some eggs, and a quart of milk. Fried chicken sounded like the perfect meal to make since the house was currently at odds and ends. Even though she had planned to make lasagne, she knew the boys would think fried chicken a treat since the only chicken Randall had ever managed was grilled—and usually overcooked.

She'd just heated up the oil and had put the first pieces of chicken in the pot when the kitchen door opened and Kaylene scampered in.

"Hi, Elizabeth! You're back."

After making sure the pot was well out of Kaylene's reach, Elizabeth turned to her. "I came to help out. My grandmother is here, too. Did you hear about Randall?"

She nodded earnestly. "Uh-huh. I wanted to come home, but my teacher said I had to wait 'cause there wasn't nothing I could do."

"I'm glad she had you wait. All we've been doing is watching Randall sleep."

"Now what are you doing?"

"Making fried chicken. Want to help?"

"Can I go see Randall first?"

"Nope. We've got to let him sleep."

Kaylene's eyes grew wide. "Nothing's gonna happen to him, is it?"

"What are you worried about?"

She bit her lip. "Nothing."

"Are you sure about that?"

Kaylene said nothing, only looked down at her bare feet.

Elizabeth looked at the little girl closely. There was a line of worry on her face. Etched clearly there, as clearly as if she was spouting off a whole list of complaints.

"Come here." When Kaylene got close, Elizabeth picked her up at the waist and swung her onto the kitchen counter.

"Lizzie, I'm not supposed to be sitting up here!"

"Maybe not. But I saw Levi sitting in this same place the other day. As far as I'm concerned, that means you can sit up here, too."

She giggled. "You're funny."

"Don't tell anyone that!"

"Why not?"

"Because everyone thinks I'm very serious, you see." When Kaylene giggled again, Elizabeth smiled. "Do me a favor and stay right there for a few minutes while I finish the chicken. Then I'll make you a snack and we can talk."

"What should I do while you're cooking?"

"You can tell me all about your day. How was school?"

"Okay."

"Just okay?"

She shrugged. "You know I'm not very smart."

"I don't know any such thing. You shouldn't talk like that."

"It's the truth. I have trouble reading. And I'm not that *gut* at math, either."

Carefully, Elizabeth pulled another two pieces of chicken out of the hot oil. "I thought Miriam was helping you with your reading."

"She did. But I still don't make the best grades. That's okay, though."

"And why is that?"

"Because we all have things we're *gut* at. Schooling isn't what I do best."

"What do you do best?"

"Art. I'm a real good artist."

"That is not something I am good at. I'd love to see some of your work. What do you like to do? Draw? Paint?"

"Draw." She took a deep breath. "But we're learning about the food chain. Want to hear all about it?"

"Of course."

Elizabeth let Kaylene's stories about school and foxes hunting rabbits float over her as she continued to fry up the chicken and place it all on a pile of old newspapers, just like her grandmother used to do back when she could see better and Elizabeth was a little girl.

"Want to hear about sea animals next? 'Cause I didn't know this, but seals eat a lot of fish."

"I want to hear all about everything," she teased.

Off Kaylene went again, telling all sorts of stories about seals and plankton, Orca whales and abalone. The nine-year-old wasn't talking in any special order. Instead, she seemed content to share as many random facts as possible.

And Elizabeth, who was so used to spending much of her day in silence, ate up the stories.

When the last of the chicken was done, Elizabeth made Kaylene some hot chocolate, then, to the little girl's delight, hopped up on the counter next to her.

"What are you going to do if everyone sees you up here?"

"I don't know. I guess I'll see if they're upset about me being up here. If they are, I'll make up an excuse."

"What kind of excuse?"

"Maybe I'll say there's a bug down there?" she teased.

"They won't think that's a *gut* reason."

"You can help me think of one."

"Maybe we saw a rat?"

In spite of their silly conversation, Elizabeth found herself shuddering. "I don't even want to joke about something like that."

Kaylene giggled. "I suppose not." After a pause, her voice turned soft. "Hey, Elizabeth?"

"Hmm?"

"Is Randall really going to be okay, do you think?"

"I think so. The doctors wouldn't have allowed him to come home if they didn't think he was going to be okay. If they were worried, they would have asked him to stay at the hospital overnight."

"He fell at his work site, you know," Kaylene said importantly. "And not only did he break his leg, but he had to get stitches, too. Maybe the doctors are wrong."

"I don't think so."

"But he is really hurt."

"Yes. But then the Lord looked out for him. The other construction men called for an ambulance, and He provided *gut* doctors and nurses to check on him. Now Randall simply needs to rest and heal."

After peeking around to see if any of her siblings were around, Kaylene said, "I'm not supposed to worry, but I was kind of afraid something was going to happen to him."

"What do you mean by that?"

She averted her eyes. "You know."

A slow, sinking feeling settled inside Elizabeth. Remembering how inconsolable she'd been when her own father had died, and how everyone had cautioned her to not talk to her *mamm* about it, she said slowly, "Kay, are you afraid Randall is going to die?"

Her eyes got wide. "Uh-huh. My parents died, you know. Both of them. My *mamm* died right after she had me."

"I know. But that wasn't your fault. You don't think it was, do you?"

She shook her head. "I used to, but Junior told me over and over that it wasn't my fault."

"He was right."

"Junior said that no one thought anything was wrong with my *mamm*, but then she died." In a soft voice, she added, "You never know what is going to happen."

Elizabeth would have given anything for Junior to be right there with them. Even she knew that this was the kind of thing that Junior had always handled in that calm, competent way of his.

But since it was just the two of them she decided to say what was in her heart. Twenty years had taught her that erring on the side of trying to do the right thing was always better than being afraid to do anything.

"That's why we have Jesus, Kaylene. We have Him so we don't have to wonder about what will happen in the future, because we know that He will take care of everything."

"Do you really believe that?"

No one had ever asked her about her faith before. Oh, someone might have asked if she believed in God when she was little. Or folks had asked her about being Amish.

But as far as asking about what was in her heart? Asking if she actually believed all the things she'd been taught to be true?

Little nine-year-old Kaylene was the very first.

"I really do," she replied softly, surprising herself with the emotion behind her words. Suddenly, it was as if the Lord himself was reminding her that He'd always been with her. And through everything she'd been through, from her father passing away to her mother falling in love with another man and ultimately moving away . . . to bearing the responsibility of her grandmother and yes, having her heart broken by Randall . . .

Through it all, she'd felt a wealth of emotions. She had felt discouraged and worried and hurt. But her faith had never wavered.

Feeling more sure of herself, she said, "I don't believe that God ever forgets us, or makes bad things happen because we did something wrong or we weren't good enough."

"Then how come I've lost lots of people?"

"I don't know," Elizabeth said, choosing each word with care. "It's the way of the world, I suppose. We are supposed to outlive our parents. That means every one of us loses our parents at one time or another. I don't know of a person who said losing a mother or father was easy." She sighed. "I don't know why you had to lose them so early, Kaylene. Only God knows that. All I do know is that while the Lord took your parents far too young, He also gave you a great big family who truly cares about you. And that is a blessing in itself."

"Everyone's been leaving me. Even Junior."

"Do you really think he has?"

"Uh-huh. He moved away. He wanted to go live with Miriam."

"It's the way of the world for everyone to start their own lives, too," she said softly. "Don't you think?"

"But I didn't want him to leave me. Even though he moved away it feels like he left me for good."

"I heard he also asked if you wanted to go live with him. Is that true?"

"Uh-huh. But I didn't think I should say yes."

"Why?"

"Because he loves Miriam now and they're gonna have a *boppli*."

"What does that have to do with you saying yes?"

Kaylene bit her lip and hesitated.

Sensing that whatever was going through the little girl's mind needed to be shared, Elizabeth pushed a bit. "You can tell me anything, Kay. I won't judge."

"I said no 'cause I don't think Junior loves me like he used to," she finally replied in a rush.

"I happen to know he still loves you very much."

"But he has Miriam now."

"God made our hearts pretty big, Kaylene. I happen to know that there's room in our hearts to love more than one person."

"You think so?"

Kaylene looked so skeptical, Elizabeth squeezed her shoulders. "Of course I do. I mean, look at you and me. I'm an only child. But you have seven siblings. Do you love all your brothers and sisters?"

"Uh-huh."

"Well, is your heart better and bigger because you have more siblings and I don't have any? Do you think I can only love a little bit?"

She rolled her eyes. "Of course not."

"Then why can't Junior love Miriam and you?"

"He's going to have a baby."

"Babies aren't too big. I bet he could fit a baby in his heart, too."

As she'd hoped, Kaylene giggled again.

"Dear, this might not be my place to say it, but I think you are making a mountain out of a molehill. I promise things aren't as bad as you seem to believe."

"Maybe not."

"Definitely not. After all, I did make fried chicken. And I make really good fried chicken. Some of the best around."

"Maybe Randall will want some?"

"Maybe. Or some soup. Are you ready to take a peek inside Randall's room now?"

"*Jah.*"

"*Gut.*" After hopping down, Elizabeth turned and helped Kaylene down. "Go down the hall, peek in, and if he's awake, pay him a visit."

She bit her bottom lip. "He might not want my company."

"You're right, he might not. Or . . . he might. He might be grumpy like one of those polar bears you were talking about. But he is going to be okay. I feel certain the Lord is looking out for him right this minute."

chapter nineteen

When Pippa sat down with both Bud and Miguel at one of the front tables in the restaurant, she made sure to face the door that led to the kitchen. She not only wanted to keep tabs on the dining room, but she figured if things got out of hand she could signal to one of the girls to help her out.

Her only consolation was that Miguel and Bud looked just as uneasy. They were seated at a square table, Miguel and Bud across from each other, and her on one side between them. Neither was looking directly at the other or at her. The tension emanating was a tangible thing—she felt like she was sitting with two strangers instead of the man she used to be married to and the man who had recently become a good friend.

"So, what did you want to talk about?" she asked impatiently. She was more than ready to have this little impromptu meeting over and done with.

To her surprise, it was Bud who started the conversation. "Miguel stopped me on the way to my car and asked me to stop seeing you."

"How did he even know we were seeing each other?"

"I told him."

"What?"

"Pippa, I wanted everything to be out in the open."

She understood that. Kind of. But bringing Miguel to her

restaurant? "If you had called, I would have asked you not to bring him."

"I decided to take a risk."

"I'm sitting right here, you know," Miguel said.

She exhaled. "We are divorced. You can no longer tell me what or what not to do."

"But that doesn't mean I want to see my friend and you together."

She felt helpless. "What do you want me to say, Bud?"

"Not a thing. Actually, all I want you to do is listen to what I'm about to tell Miguel." Before Miguel could interrupt, Bud continued, his voice firm. "It's like this," he said. "For years, we've known each other and have been good friends. You met Pippa first. And because of that, I stayed to one side when you asked her out. But I knew even back then that I liked her."

Pippa was floored. "You did?"

He cast an embarrassed smile her way. "I did."

"I never knew."

"I couldn't let you know. You were with Miguel."

"That's right," Miguel interjected. "She was mine." He glared at her. "Don't you even start pretending that you didn't love me. We said vows."

"I did love you. But even back then I wasn't sure." She couldn't even believe she was admitting this now! "But, Miguel, it had to be as obvious to you as it was to me that things weren't progressing like they should. Instead of becoming closer when we got married, we drifted apart."

"You were always working."

"And you were always with your friends."

"And Bud was one of them."

"I wasn't married to her. You can't blame me for your actions."

All of this talking was well and good, but she sure wasn't eager to rehash everything that had already been said a dozen times. "Are we done?"

Bud shook his head. "Just give me a sec," he said gently. "Miguel, I'm telling you now that I intend to keep seeing Pippa as long as she'll have me. You are going to need to learn to accept that."

"And if I don't?"

"Then I'll move, and we won't be friends anymore."

"You'd do that, Bud?" Pippa could hardly believe what he was saying. It was beyond anything she could have imagined, certainly beyond anything she imagined anyone saying to her.

Bud looked at her directly and kept looking at her, even though Miguel was looking more furious by the second. "Yeah. I passed up my chance once before. I'm not about to pass it up again."

Miguel surged to his feet. "I don't have to sit here and listen to this."

Bud got to his feet, too. "You're right, you don't. But you do have to honor Pippa's choices."

Miguel shook his head slowly. "You're asking too much of me, Bud."

"You need to calm down."

"I can't calm down. How did you think I was going to react? You were my friend."

Bud stiffened. "Were?"

"If you continue to see Pippa, I want you to know that our friendship is over."

"You're being unreasonable."

"No, you are being a child." He mumbled a couple of choice Spanish words under his breath—words that Pippa sincerely hoped no one else in the restaurant could understand. "I don't know what you thought was going to happen here. I have no idea how you thought I was going to react."

And with that, he turned and walked out of the restaurant without another word.

Bud sighed as he sat down. "Well, that went well," he said dryly.

As Pippa became aware that they'd drawn quite an audience, she pressed her hands to her face. "I can't even believe this all just happened," she mumbled. "I was really hoping I wouldn't have to see Miguel again anytime soon."

"Please don't be mad at me. I wanted everything out in the open."

"I'm not mad."

"I wouldn't blame you if you were. But it had to be done, Pippa."

"Did it? I don't even know what to think right now. I'm not even sure if I know how I feel." She shrugged.

"Pippa, I don't want to sneak around with you. I don't want there to be any confusion, either. I want to date you. I'm serious about you."

Those were words she would have loved to have heard when she was young. Even two years ago, back before things with Miguel had gotten so bad, she probably would have reacted to Bud's sweet words differently than she was at the moment.

Now? She felt too cynical. Too tired. She'd learned the

hard way that words were easy to say. Sometimes, it was actions that mattered.

But that was exactly what Bud had done. He'd gotten them all together, and had been willing to have her face Miguel in order for her to see just how serious he was about their relationship.

"I guess I'm feeling a little stunned, if you want to know the truth."

Bud winced. "That wasn't quite the reaction that I was hoping for."

"To be honest, I'm feeling a lot of things. So much, I don't even trust myself. But I'll give you this, you are full of surprises."

To her amusement, he seemed pleased by that. "I'll take stunned. Please, just don't be too mad at me."

She thought about it for a moment. Was she mad? It certainly seemed like she should be! But, actually, what she was feeling had a lot more to do with regrets than anger. She wished she had known about Bud being interested in her before she and Miguel had gotten so serious. She wished she had known that he would have stood up for her, placed her first in his life before now.

Correction: She wished she had believed that there were men like him before she'd made such a mess of her life.

But if there was one thing she did know, it was that she would never regret what had just happened. Not even for one minute.

"I'm not mad."

"Will you still let me take you home?"

The question hung in the air. She wanted to grasp it, but was afraid if she moved forward she was going to want more and more.

Setting herself up to be disappointed. Or maybe, just maybe . . . she was also setting herself up to be happy.

"Let me go get my purse and tell everyone good-bye," she said as she stood up. "Then, I'll be ready to leave with you."

"Good. That's real good, Pippa."

Funny, she felt the same exact way.

chapter twenty

Hours later, after making fried chicken, a green salad, mashed potatoes, and a corn casserole for supper . . .

After joining the Beiler boys, Kaylene, and her grandmother at the table and quickly eating a generous slice of dried apple pie topped off by a too-big scoop of vanilla ice cream . . .

And after laughing with Levi at the sink while he helped her with the dishes, and chiding Neil for sneaking another slice of pie . . .

Elizabeth collapsed on the couch in the hearth room. Glad they kept such a casual house, she propped her feet on the coffee table and silently vowed to herself that she wouldn't move until it was time to get ready for bed.

When Micah walked by, a textbook and spiral notebook in his hands, he smiled. "You look comfortable."

"I am. Ah, you don't mind my feet on the table, do you?"

"You know how we live. Do you think we'd ever mind that?"

She laughed. "That's why I went ahead and did it."

"If you keep making supper like you did tonight, you can do pretty much whatever you want."

"I won't tell Randall you said that."

He grinned. "*Gut.* I need to do a little reading. Do you mind some company?"

"I don't mind. But it is your *haus*, Micah. You don't need to ask me."

Micah tilted his head. "You know what? I was just thinking about that."

"Oh?"

He tossed his books on the coffee table and plopped down on the big leather recliner across from her. "You and Anna Mae gave us something special tonight."

"Micah. I made fried chicken. That isn't too special."

"We both know I'm talking about you making this big house feel like a home. It was nice."

"*Danke*. I've already talked to Neil about this, but I really am grateful you didn't mind my grandmother coming here, too."

"She's a lot of fun." He paused. "I almost like her being here the most of all."

She chuckled. "If you were trying to get a rise out of me, you made a mistake there. I happen to think she's pretty terrific myself." Wanting the focus to be away from her, she gestured to the books. "What are you studying tonight?"

"Biology."

"You and Kaylene! Have you been reading about the food chain?"

"I wish I was only learning about the food chain. This chapter is on photosynthesis and its effects on the global climate."

She lifted her chin. "See that? You just went over my head."

"Sorry. It's interesting, though. I like it, but not as much as my other class. I'm taking American history, too."

"What are you going to do with all that learning, Micah?"

"I can't decide. Sometimes I feel like I'm meant to stay

on the path I'm on. That I'm meant to go to college and get a degree. Other times, I can't help but think of one of our uncles. He's Amish, but he's also one of the smartest men I've ever met. He reads about things like I'm reading for fun."

"When do you think you'll know?"

He shrugged. "If there's one good thing about not having parents at my age, it's that I don't have one of them telling me what to do. I figure I have all the time I need. As long as I do my part around here, you know."

"From what I've seen, you do a lot."

"I try." He gazed at her then, a new light of concern in his eyes. "Elizabeth, what is going on with you and Randall? Are you two still seeing each other?"

"You know I just saw him a couple of hours ago," she teased.

"You know what I mean. Do you want to start seeing him again?"

That felt like a loaded question, one that she couldn't give a straight answer to. All things considered, she would have rather avoided it entirely. Maybe even pushed Micah's question away.

But he was staring at her intently, as if her answer really mattered to him. "I don't know," she hedged. "Micah, you know that your brother and I don't seem to be communicating very well these days."

"Has he upset you?"

Because he looked like he was ready to do battle on her behalf, she shook her head. "Not at all." She shrugged. "It's just hard not to feel like we had our chance. It wasn't meant to be." Though she didn't believe her words, she felt like that's how Randall felt about things.

"For what it's worth, I know that he was right fond of you.

Randall's not one to talk too much about his personal life, but I do know that you meant a lot to him."

It didn't escape her notice that they were speaking about her and Randall in the past tense. The realization made her sad, but not as devastated as she used to feel. Maybe she was growing up?

Or, perhaps, she had simply learned to move on?

"Micah, if it's all the same to you, I'd rather not talk about me and Randall anymore."

After staring at her for a few seconds, he exhaled. "Of course." Leaning forward, he picked up his book. "I'll go in the kitchen and leave you alone."

"Please, don't do that. It's time I went to bed. See you in the morning."

"Yes, you will. *Gut naught*."

As she slowly walked up the stairs and settled into what was Claire's old bedroom, Elizabeth felt a new sense of calm. At last, she'd finally turned the corner. She and her grandmother were going to stay here a few days, watch over Randall, clean and dust and cook as much as possible, and get paid a pretty penny for it.

Then they were going to return home and pretend that their quiet, empty house felt as comfortable and warm as the Beilers'. That she was glad to not be living in the middle of a bunch of noisy men who had never met a clean floor that they couldn't make dirty.

As she clutched her nightgown to her chest, Elizabeth knew if she tried really hard, she might even be able to fool herself for a while into believing it, too.

After swallowing two ibuprofen tablets, Judith leaned back

with a moan. "Mamm, I'm so sore and achy, I feel like I fell down a flight of stairs. I don't know what's wrong with me."

"I do. You have the flu, Judith," her mother replied. "And though it pains me to remind you of this, I hope you recall that I told you to get some rest two days ago when you started to look a little peaked."

"Mamm, mothers don't get sick."

She chuckled. "They most certainly do!"

"Well, they don't let everyone know it. I can't remember a single day when we were little that you stayed in bed all day."

"Just because you don't remember it doesn't mean it didn't happen."

"Still—"

"Oh, but you've become a trial! Judith Knox, if you don't lie down and get some rest, you're going to infect the rest of the family."

Trying to breathe through a stuffy nose, Judith waved off her mother's words. "You're overreacting, Mamm."

"I think not." Holding up the thermometer, she said, "The evidence is right here, one hundred and two point two. You're sick."

If she hadn't felt so achy and miserable, Judith knew she would have protested a bit more. Instead, she coughed. "How is James?"

Her mother's gaze softened. "He is *gut*. Caleb and Rebecca have him for the day. Then Gretta and Josh are going to watch him tonight."

"But Ben—"

"Ben spent some time with him this morning, and he'll visit with him for a bit this afternoon. But he is needed here, I think."

"I don't need him to fetch and carry for me. He needs to

be with the baby." To her shame, tears filled her eyes. Impatiently, she swiped at them. She was so tired of being needy! "I'm fine."

"I wish you were, but you are not."

"But what if Bernie discovers that I'm not with James?"

"If I were her, I would be praising the Lord that you had the good sense to stay away from him for the time being."

"Mamm!"

"I'm only speaking the truth. You don't want James to get sick, do you?"

She was teetering between that place where she knew her mother was right and admitting out loud that she was right. "*Nee*, Mamm."

She opened one bleary eye just in time to see her mother smile in a self-satisfied way. "Now, I am going to make you some soup and do a little bit of cleaning while you rest."

"You don't need to clean my *haus*."

"I happen to disagree. Everything's a mess, dear. Go to sleep."

As she listened to her mother walk down the hall into the kitchen, Judith thought about getting up and taking a shower. Instead, she rolled over and went back to sleep.

Hopefully she would be feeling better before Bernie ever found out that she'd been neglecting James's needs for a whole day.

She needed to be as perfect a foster mother as she could be. She needed to do anything it took to keep James as long as possible.

chapter twenty-one

There was nothing like sitting alone in a room and feeling completely helpless. Randall stared at the door and silently willed it to open, hopefully by one of his brothers. He needed to go to the bathroom.

Nothing.

He drummed his fingers. Eyed the cowbell Neil had brought in for him to use in an emergency. Of course, he'd meant it as a joke. Beilers were nothing if not self-sufficient; losing their parents had instilled in them a can-do attitude. They didn't ask for help unless it was for Kaylene.

And if for some reason they were desperate for a little help, well, they certainly didn't ring bells when they needed a helping hand—they yelled. But Elizabeth and her grandmother were in the house. It seemed pretty rude to yell for them to come to his room.

He shifted. Wished he hadn't drunk all that water.

Well, there was a time for pride, and a time when one didn't want to wet the bed. With a feeling of abject resignation, he curved his hand around the cowbell. Picked it up. Mentally prepared himself to start clanging the thing. . . .

"Ah, you're awake!"

His head snapped around, and he realized his mortification was complete. Anna Mae Nolt was peering into the room, her weathered face looking as kind as ever.

And her dark brown eyes were staring at that bell in his hand with a surprisingly wise expression. "Looks like you're needing something. What is it?"

"Is one of my brothers around, Anna Mae?"

"*Nee.* Levi is at work. Neil and Micah are in the fields today with a pair of young boys they hired on." Still staring at that cowbell, she raised her brows. "Now, what may I help you with?"

"Oh. Well. Maybe Elizabeth could come in?"

"I'll go see if she can. She was down in your basement washing clothes, though, so she might not be able to come upstairs for some time."

This was awful. Beyond awful, even venturing into horrible territory. "Could you tell her that it's important? Please?"

To his dismay, she stepped inside. "I may be old but I'm not helpless. What do you need? Spit it out now."

"I need help walking to the bathroom." Keeping his eyes firmly averted he said, "I can't put any weight on my leg."

"Oh. Well, now. To be sure, I can see how that might present a problem."

He could, too. He also knew he would never forget this feeling of embarrassment. "I hate to be a pest, but Anna Mae, could you please go get Elizabeth? Quickly?"

"Certainly, dear."

When she turned away, looking more than a little amused, he closed his eyes. He could only hope that it would be years before any of his siblings heard about this. "Lord, I am sure you are putting me through this for a *gut* reason," he mumbled. "But I have to tell ya, I wish I knew why you felt I needed to be humiliated this way."

"Knock, knock," Elizabeth said as she walked in. "I heard you needed some help?"

He sighed. Swallowing his pride, he nodded. *"Jah.* Help me walk to the bathroom, wouldja?"

While she walked toward the bed, he shifted to the side of the mattress. Even that small movement made him clench his teeth. Last night when Levi had helped him, the pain relievers he'd been given at the hospital must have still been in his system.

"Randall, are you going to be able to do this?"

"I don't have a choice."

She looked doubtful. "Um, maybe we could find a way for you to use a bedpan or something?"

"Don't even think about that." Raising his arm, he glared at her. "It's hard enough having to ask your grandmother to go get you. Now come over here and help me to my feet."

Her lips twitched. "I had no idea you would be so grumpy."

"You'd be grumpy, too, if you had to ask for help to get out of bed," he said as he draped his arm around her shoulders. "Okay, you ready?"

"As I'll ever be." She wrapped an arm around his waist. "One, two, three. Umph!"

At last, he was on his feet. After teetering a little bit, he finally got his balance. With a sigh, he lifted his leg and half hopped toward the door. By the time they reached the hall, he was afraid he was putting the majority of his two hundred pounds on her shoulder. "Am I hurting you?"

"Not at all. Come now, Randall. Just a few more steps."

An eternity later, they reached the door to the bathroom. "I won't be long," he said as he grabbed hold of the counter-top and used it to brace his weight.

"Are you going to be okay in there?"

"I'll be fine," he muttered as he closed the door in her face. He was dizzy and hurting and pretty unsteady on his feet. But really, there were just some things a man had to do unassisted.

As she stood on the other side of the door, Elizabeth realized two things. The first was that she was stronger than she'd realized. She would never tell Randall—at least not anytime soon—but he was a big man and he weighed a ton. While he'd been doing his best to hop and act as if he wasn't in pain, she'd been praying that he didn't fall. There would have been no way she could have held his whole weight.

The other realization was a whole lot harder to swallow. She'd been lying something awful to Micah last night. Seeing Randall in bed completely helpless and grumpily asking for help had stolen her heart.

It seemed that she was still in love with Randall.

When she heard the water in the sink turn on, she leaned a little closer, then grinned when he opened the door, looking like a new man. His face was damp, too.

To her dismay, he looked just as handsome as ever. Maybe even more so, because he looked slightly scruffy. Randall was by no means the type of man who fussed over himself, but just now she realized that he was the type of man who took care with his appearance. His nails were always clean and neatly trimmed, his cheeks free of stubble.

And, she realized, back when they were courting, he'd always smelled like fresh soap and some kind of evergreen shampoo.

As a whiff of the soap's scent hit her hard, her body reacted. She leaned a little closer to him, all of her senses on alert.

Afraid he would notice that she was practically sniffing him, she primly folded her hands in front of her apron. "Looks like you washed up a bit?" she said as she positioned herself under his shoulder and they began their journey back to his bedroom.

"Yeah. I brushed my teeth and at least tried to wash my face." He grimaced. "I hate feeling so out of it."

"I know, but that isn't what matters now. We need to concentrate on your leg," she said when they got to the side of his bed again.

He sat down with a sigh. "This mattress has never felt so good."

"I imagine it has not." Leaning close, she fluffed his pillows and helped him get arranged. He moved to accommodate her.

And then, just like that, they were face-to-face. His eyes widened as her lips parted, though whether she was thinking about kissing him or protesting him being in her space, she didn't know.

All she did notice was that Randall had shifted his attention to her lips and that her breath had quickened.

And that it was all taking place on his bed.

Before she did something foolish like touch him in a more personal manner, she pulled back with a jerk. "How about some macaroni and cheese?"

"Pardon?"

"I made you some macaroni and cheese. Want some?"

"Yeah. That sounds great."

She turned away and practically raced to the door. "I'll be back shortly. Want some iced tea or water?"

"Either is fine. And hey, Beth?"

She pivoted on her heel. "What?"

"*Danke.*" He smiled sheepishly. "You know, for coming to my rescue."

"It was my pleasure," she said automatically. As their eyes

met and she realized how awkward that sounded, she stumbled over her words. "I mean. I was glad I was here. I mean, oh, I don't know what I mean. I'm going to be going now. But I'll be back soon with your food."

He smiled. "I'll look forward to it."

If she wasn't so terribly embarrassed, she would have thought he was flirting with her.

She turned abruptly and hurried back down the stairs and into the kitchen.

"How he's doing?" Mommi asked. "Feeling better?"

Elizabeth chuckled. "I tell you what, I thought girls were prudes, but that Randall Beiler takes the cake. You would have thought he was the first person in Sugarcreek to have to go to the bathroom."

Her grandmother's lips twitched. "I must say his bashfulness took me by surprise, too. But at least you were home."

She pulled out a bowl. "Have you seen a tray? I'm going to bring him some macaroni and cheese."

"I have." Looking pleased, she pointed to a cabinet. "I hope the Beilers won't be mad, but I decided to clean out this cabinet. Inside are all sorts of linens and old serving dishes. Everything was in disarray so I've been washing the old trays and putting everything back in a more organized way."

Elizabeth took the tray. "You don't think they'll be upset, thinking that we're getting into their private business?"

"They asked you here to cook and clean, Lizzie. That's what I'm doing. Stop worrying so much."

"All right. I'll try," she murmured as she walked back upstairs.

But privately, she wondered if it was a mistake to make themselves so at home in the Beilers' house.

chapter twenty-two

When it rained, it poured, Judith decided as she wearily padded to the front door to let in Bernie, who had arrived on an unannounced visit.

As usual, Bernie had a packed tote bag, reading glasses perched on the top of her head, and a cell phone in her hand. But when she got a good look at Judith, her welcoming expression faded into a worried frown. "Judith, you look awful!"

"I know. I'm sick."

"What's wrong, dear?"

"I've got the flu." Practically hugging the door, she cautioned, "I'm not sure that you want to come in." A little burst of hope ballooned inside her. Maybe her illness would be just the thing to ward off any bad news that Bernie was bringing with her. "Perhaps you could come back in a few days?"

Bernie did look like she wished she was anywhere else. But after a moment's hesitation, she walked inside. "I'm afraid this can't wait. I have some news."

"Come on in, then." She rubbed her arms over the fuzzy cardigan she'd slipped over her dress. "Let's go to the kitchen. It's warmer back there."

When they sat at the kitchen table, she was especially glad for Ben. He'd cleaned the whole kitchen before he left for the store. Otherwise, Bernie would have been treated to a sink and countertops full of dirty dishes.

The moment Bernie sat down, she pulled on her glasses and started rummaging through her tote bag. Judith noticed that her movements seemed a bit frantic, her expression pained. Judith watched Bernie open the files, rearrange them, then rearrange them again, as if she needed to do something with her hands.

At last, she stopped, then looked around the kitchen. "Where's James?"

"He's not here."

Bernie's brows rose. " Where is he?"

The alarm she'd been doing her best to keep at bay rose up in a frightening way. "My *mamm* took him to my brother and sister-in-law's *haus*."

"You didn't inform me of this."

"We didn't realize we had to." Folding her arms across her chest, Judith added, "I had a high fever. We didn't want him to get sick."

"I see."

"Bernie, I do not. What is wrong?"

Laying both of her hands flat on the table, Bernie looked at Judith directly. "There's no easy way to say this. Kendra passed away last night."

The shock, combined with the sight of Bernie's tear-filled eyes, spurred her tears, too. A dozen questions entered her head, the first of which was why and how. But the words stuck in her throat, her questions fading, compared to the hurt she was feeling. Poor Kendra, dying in prison, away from her family and friends.

And poor little James. If there was one thing Judith was completely certain about, it was that Kendra had loved her baby very much. Now the boy was going to grow up never knowing that love.

Belatedly realizing that Bernie was waiting for her to make some kind of response, Judith sighed. "This is heartbreaking, Bernie."

The social worker tossed her glasses on the table and dug in her tote bag once again. When she pulled out a packet of tissues, she wiped her eyes. "I still can't believe it. I heard the news late last night and spent this morning trying to learn what happened."

"Did you find out anything?"

Bernie nodded. "Kendra developed some complications. A fever spiked, she slid into unconsciousness, and then her heart stopped beating." Swiping her eyes again, she said, "I can hardly believe it."

"It seems the Lord was impatient for her to join him in heaven."

Bernie stilled. "Do you really think that?"

"I hope so," Judith said, slowly realizing that she did, indeed, believe those words wholeheartedly. "It's not for us to try to understand why things happen," she added, realizing right then and there that her mother had said this to her time and again when she'd been recovering from her miscarriage. "I will admit that wanting to believe something and accepting it are two different things. It's faith to give up one's power to God. But it's easier if you do. He has it anyway, you see."

With a little sniff, Bernie reached out and clasped one of Judith's hands in her own. "I can't believe this. All night I wondered how I was going to be able to tell you the news. And I've been so angry. Kendra had made mistakes, but she was so young. She had a whole lifetime to be the person she wanted to be."

Grabbing one of Bernie's tissues, Judith swiped at her

eyes. "I might understand, but it still makes me terribly sad." After another sniff, she said, "How does this affect James's future?"

"That is the other reason why I came over so early, Judith. Kendra's sisters are really struggling with Kendra's sudden death. They want to see James as soon as possible."

"How soon, do you think?"

"Judith, they asked to come over here tomorrow."

"What? But I thought Kendra was going to make her feelings known."

"I'm still investigating, but whether she wrote a note or not, as of this morning, her sisters want to contest her wishes. I'm to escort them to meet James and you and Ben tomorrow."

"Couldn't you ask them for at least one more day? I'm sick, Bernie. Truly, I am."

"I'll do what I can, but there's a strong possibility that they won't care about that. They're impatient. I think if they could have arranged things, they would have tried to come to Sugarcreek today."

"And I'm not allowed to have any say in when they get to come over here?"

"Not without getting a lawyer." Her expression pained, Bernie added, "I know this is a shock and it doesn't seem fair. But we have no choice. They've already contacted a lawyer. Judith, they want custody of James, and from what they've been saying so far, they're willing to do just about everything they can think of to get him."

As Judith stared at Bernie in shock, she felt everything she'd worked so hard to attain fall away. Her composure, her hope. Her dignity. Her sense of peace.

All she felt at the moment was a deep sense of hurt mixed in with a good portion of bitterness and dismay.

Right this second, it didn't matter if she truly believed that God was in control or not.

All she really knew was that if she lost custody of James, she wasn't going to care for His decisions.

And she should have remembered that, when she thought things were bad, why, they could always get worse.

Randall had now been in bed for the majority of the last three days. After today's visit to the doctor, he was relieved to know that while he was going to be bedridden for at least one more week, it didn't look as if surgery was going to be necessary.

In addition, his new fiberglass cast was a marked improvement from the temporary one. Now he didn't feel as if he could do permanent damage if he turned the wrong way in his sleep.

He was sitting in bed, trying to get interested in either a farming magazine—courtesy of Neil—or a mystery—courtesy of Micah—when Levi popped his head in.

"Care for some company?"

"More than anything. I'm not tired enough to sleep, but too tired to read."

Levi sauntered in and sat on the side of his bed, his bare feet swinging off the side of the mattress. "I'm pretty sure that no one would want to read either of those choices. You should have gotten something else to do."

"Like what?"

"I don't know . . . cards?"

When they were far smaller, he and his brothers had spent many an evening playing UNO. Then they'd moved on to hearts, and finally poker. Junior had learned to play from one of his English friends, and it had been exciting to do something forbidden.

The memories brought a smile to his face. "Me and Junior sure had some good times when we were supposed to be sleeping."

"You hardly ever played with me."

"That's because you were so much younger."

"How about I bring in a deck of cards later?" Looking especially mischievous, he added, "We can play for pennies."

"Deal." He stretched his arms. "How's everything at the job site?"

"Abraham still feels real bad about your fall. You're not supposed to know about this, but he's started a fund for you. He's collecting some money to help pay for your expenses."

"That's real nice of him, though it wasn't his fault. My foot slipped."

"I've never known you to slip or fall, ever."

"There's a first time for everything, I suppose." Rubbing one of the abrasions on his arm that was almost healed, he added, "It's my fault. I've been up on those joists so often I became a little too cocky. I should have been concentrating more on my safety. Let that be a lesson to you, little brother."

"I'll try to remember that."

"*Gut.*" He hoped his expression matched his tone, because he had just remembered what he had been thinking about when he'd fallen—one Elizabeth Nolt.

"You know what? I think Lizzie and her grandmother have settled right in," Levi said, just as if he'd read Randall's mind.

"Oh? What have they been doing?"

"What haven't they been doing! Anna Mae cleaned out Mamm's old cupboard."

"What one is that?"

"You know the one. The one that had all her trays and cups and saucers." Grinning, he said, "Listen to this: At first Anna Mae was worried that we might not want anyone fussing with our things."

"It's been more like none of us ever wanted to peer inside." Just thinking about the dark secrets that had lain hidden in the back of that cupboard for years and years made him shudder. "How awful was it?"

"I don't know. When Elizabeth showed it to me, everything inside was sparkling clean and neatly organized. It could have been in Miriam's kitchen."

"I guess that will be money well spent, then."

Levi nodded. "Elizabeth said it was *gut* that they have been living with us. She said if she'd been here alone and had to clean out dirty cupboards like that, she'd have to charge a pretty penny."

Though it made no sense, his feelings were a little hurt. He'd thought they'd gone beyond her thinking of his family as just a job. "She said that?"

"I think she was joking." He stretched his legs. "Anyway, I think they're real happy here. Anna Mae said she likes all the commotion. Said it's too quiet at her house."

"I guess it would be a change."

"Hey, you okay?"

"Yeah. I'm just getting tired again. I think I'm going to take a nap."

Levi scrambled off the bed. "I'll let Elizabeth know."

"Why does she need to know?" Why did everything go back to that girl?

"Because she was about to come in and bring you something to eat. Now I'll tell her to wait."

"You can tell her to bring me something."

"No, I think I'm going to ask her to wait. You're far too grumpy to be around the rest of us," he said with a hurt expression in his eyes. "Honestly, Randall, you're worse than Junior ever was when he was stuck on Miriam."

"I'm not stuck on Elizabeth."

"Uh-huh."

"I'm not. She and I are through."

"You just keep telling yourself that, *bruder*," Levi said as he left the room. "Maybe one day we'll all believe it."

The moment Levi closed his door, Randall tossed the farming magazine on the floor and punched his pillow.

Something needed to be done about him and Elizabeth. They couldn't continue as they were, each wondering if they were about to get back together or drift even further apart.

However, this needed to be done in their own time frame, and not with his whole family in the middle of it all.

Not while he was stuck in bed.

What they needed was some time to talk about things and the space in order to do it. Which meant that it was time to ask her to leave.

chapter twenty-three

"Whatever you do, don't go see Randall for an hour or two," Levi said as he walked through the kitchen.

Looking at the tray she'd just prepared for him, filled with Swiss steak, peas and carrots, and homemade rolls, Elizabeth frowned. "What am I supposed to do with this, then?"

"I'll eat it," Kaylene said from her spot at the kitchen table, where she was dipping pretzel sticks in white chocolate and then in assorted candies.

Her grandmother shook her head. "As much as it would please me to see you eat everything on that plate, you need to wait until it's supper time."

"When is that?"

"One hour."

"Forever."

Anna Mae lifted her chin to meet Elizabeth's eye. "It's easy to forget how slow time goes through a child's eye."

"Maybe you should try one of your finished pretzel sticks, Kaylene. You know, simply to tide you over until suppertime."

When the little girl promptly picked one up and chomped on the end, Elizabeth smiled. "How does it taste?"

"*Wunderbaar.*"

"When you finish that, you need to wash your hands and then do your chores."

"Can't you do them for me?"

"I could, but I'm afraid your brothers would get mad at me for doing them."

"I wouldn't tell them."

"But I would," her grandmother said. "Your brothers are all doing extra chores because Junior is out of town and Randall is hurt. You mustn't be selfish, child."

For a split second, Kaylene's bottom lip popped out, looking for all the world like she was about to argue, then she scooted off her chair, washed her hands, and ran out of the room.

Elizabeth observed her in a bit of awe. "Mommi, you're amazing."

"*Nee*, child," she said as she pointed to the doorway. "I believe it is Junior who is."

Startled, Elizabeth swirled around. "You're back!"

"We got home late last night. How's our patient?"

"The doctor said he won't need surgery and gave him a permanent cast."

"That's mighty *gut* news."

"Levi said he was sleeping, though, so if you came to see him, you might be out of luck."

"I came by to see how you two ladies were doing. Miriam said she could spend the day over here if you're eager to leave."

"Already?"

"You've already been here four days. I have a feeling it's probably about three days longer than you wanted to be here. I know our clan can be a handful."

"Not for me," Anna Mae said. "I've enjoyed being around a big family again. And of course, spending time with Kaylene has been a delight."

"When she's not taking advantage of you."

"She's been a good girl." For a moment, Elizabeth considered telling Junior that she would be happy to stay longer, but what was the point?

She was still going to have to eventually leave. And no good was going to come out of becoming more attached to life in the Beiler household. Things between her and Randall were up in the air.

Just when he'd make it plain that anything romantic between them was long gone, he'd smile at her, they'd exchange a few flirty words, and then she would be more confused than ever.

"If Miriam could take my place, that would be good," she said finally. "I am anxious to return home, and both of us are ready to return to our own beds."

While her grandmother raised her eyebrows, Junior stared at her long and hard. At last, he nodded. "I'm glad I stopped by. I didn't want another hour to go by without making sure everything was settled between us."

While Elizabeth gaped at him, because there was no reason she could discern that everything wasn't settled, Junior pulled out his wallet.

As she watched, embarrassment making fast friends with the knowledge that she had bills to pay, Junior reached inside the leather billfold and pulled out several one-hundred-dollar bills. "Neil and I talked, and we thought this amount would cover your time here."

Her hand hovered over the money before she accepted it. "*Danke.* I appreciate this."

"Don't thank me. We owe you this. As far as I'm concerned, you earned every penny." With that adorable smile that he was so famous for, Junior continued, "Don't forget,

Claire and Beverly and I managed things between the three of us for years. As far as I'm concerned, you two have been doing the work of three."

Her grandmother held up her hands. "Please, don't include me in that. I've only been helping out where I could."

"It's all appreciated. Now, I suppose I better go check in on Randall."

"Don't wake him up."

He winked. "Don't worry, Elizabeth. He's annoying, but he's still my little brother. I won't wake him from his nap."

When he left the room, it was as if all the air had been sucked out of the room. Elizabeth sat down with a sigh. "That Junior is a force of nature. I've known him for years, of course. But until now, I've never really noticed how hard he works to keep his family running smoothly."

Mommi's eyes narrowed. "You do realize that you and him aren't that different, don't you?"

"Of course we're not alike. He has seven brothers and sisters to look after."

"You have me."

"Mommi, it's not like that. We have each other."

Her lips pursed. "I don't feel good about watching you take that money."

"I earned it honestly. We earned it."

"Child, you and I both know that you would have done the exact same thing as a favor for them. It's in your nature to want to help others."

Afraid their voices would carry, Elizabeth lowered hers. "It's also in my nature to pay my bills. This will allow me to do so. And I have to admit that I am going to feel mighty proud when I pay the bills on time this month."

"Of course, dear. Forgive me. I seem to be always saying the wrong thing these days."

Feeling more uncomfortable than ever, Elizabeth stood up. "There's nothing to forgive. I love you, Mommi." She clapped her hands together. "Now, how about we make a chocolate cake before we leave? I've yet to meet a group of men who like desserts as much as these Beilers."

"I'll get out the eggs, butter, and sugar."

As the tension between them eased, Elizabeth got busy measuring flour and baking chocolate. And finally admitted to herself that her grandmother hadn't said the wrong things at all.

Actually, she'd been exactly right.

The buzzer on the top of Pippa's stove went off at the same time that Bud knocked at her apartment's front door.

"Just a minute," she called out as she reached for the timer and turned it off.

On her way to the door, she couldn't resist pausing to look at her reflection in the antique mirror that hung in her entryway.

Yet again.

She'd bought a new dress for the dinner. It was blue cotton and had short sleeves. It was deceptively modest, though it fit her like a glove, showing off her figure.

Of course, she'd already taken it off two times that afternoon, switching to her usual uniform of jeans and a T-shirt. But in the end, she decided to err on the side of dressing up too much instead of too little.

The worst thing that could happen was that Bud would think she went to a lot of trouble for him. Which she had.

Looking at herself critically, she smoothed back her long black hair and wished, as always, it had a bit less curl. But of course there was nothing she could do about it.

Just as she couldn't help her giddiness when she prepared to open the door. Tonight she was cooking for Bud. It was a real date, just the two of them.

Bud knocked on the door again. "Pippa?"

After unlocking the deadbolt, she pulled the door open wide. And there was Bud, dressed in a blue button-down and a pair of khakis. "Hi," she said, her smile growing wider when she saw he held a bouquet of tulips.

"Hi. You look really pretty, Pippa."

"Thanks." Gesturing to his outfit, she said, "I guess we both decided to dress up a little."

"Yeah." Looking adorably bashful, he kind of thrust the flowers at her. "Here."

She took them as she led the way inside. "What a nice surprise, Bud," she said as she started opening cupboards, hoping she still had that glass vase she'd picked up at a yard sale a couple of months ago.

"I thought I should have something for you. You know, to mark the occasion."

Holding the vase she'd just filled with water, she set it slowly on the countertop. "It feels that way for you, too?"

"Very much so. I feel like we've come a long way to reach this point, Pippa."

As she looked at the dozen pink and yellow tulips in the vase, each one in a different stage of bloom, she couldn't believe how far they had come.

"I thought we were through when you showed up at the restaurant with Miguel."

His gaze softened. "Maybe I shouldn't have done that,

but after everything you went through with Miguel, I didn't want there to be any questions or secrets between us."

She gestured to the table, set with crisp white place mats and napkins. Just two hours earlier, she'd stared at it in doubt, wondering if she'd done too much. Now she thought the new place mats and carefully arranged silverware looked pretty perfect.

"Please, sit down," she said, feeling a bit like a hostess out of a Hallmark movie. "I made chicken enchiladas. I hope you like Mexican food?"

Grinning at her, he nodded. "To be honest, I like anything Mexican. Especially pretty girls named Pippa who wear amazing blue dresses."

Meeting his gaze, she stilled. Yes, they had definitely moved forward. And she had a pretty good idea that from now on, there would be no turning back.

chapter twenty-four

He'd suffered through a lot of complaints and more than a couple snide comments. But in the end, Randall had gotten his way. He was now dressed in flannel pajama bottoms, one sock, and a blue shirt. He was also attempting to rest on the couch in the keeping room.

His leg was propped on a pillow and he almost felt like himself.

Kaylene had positioned herself on the opposite end of the couch and was currently writing her name on his cast with a thick black permanent marker. "Am I supposed to write anything besides my name on your leg, Randall?"

"What else would you write?"

"I don't know." She chewed on her bottom lip for a moment. "Something like 'have a nice day'?"

Levi scoffed. "You don't write things like that, silly. You write something like 'hope you feel better.' "

"Or just write your name. Don't forget, you've already told me that you hope I feel better," Randall said in his most helpful voice. Honestly, if he didn't attempt to put some parameters around it she was going to be perched next to his foot all day.

"I think I'm going to just write 'Kaylene Beiler.' "

"He already knows who you are, Kay," Levi said with a smile. "You are goofy."

"I'm not. I'm not goofy am I, Randall?"

Eager to gain some peace, he said, "Levi was only teasin' ya, Kay. He wasn't being mean. But I don't think you're goofy at all."

"See?" She glared at Levi.

Randall looked toward Elizabeth in the kitchen. She was carefully wiping down the counters. When she met his gaze, he called out, "Elizabeth, come in here and help me out."

"I'm afraid I don't know if I'll be able to do that, Randall. I'm cleaning the kitchen, you see."

Her voice was light, and it was obvious that she was only pretending to be teasing. But there was an edge to her voice as well. "Elizabeth, all you've been doing all night is cleaning. Isn't it time to take a break?"

"I will. I'm simply trying to get everything done before I go."

"Go? Where are you going?"

"I'm going home tomorrow."

"What?" He looked around the room, at Levi, who was glaring at him, to Micah, who'd been reading one of his textbooks in the far corner, to Kaylene, who was making the tail of her *y* into a fancy curlicue. Not a one of them looked surprised. "Did all of you already know this?"

Kaylene nodded. "Uh-huh."

"We talked about it at supper," Micah said absently. "While you were in your room."

"But don't you think we need to talk about this?"

"I already talked about things with Junior," Elizabeth said after a lengthy pause. "He paid me, too, so I'm all taken care of."

She'd been paid. She'd been taken care of. Her voice was brisk and businesslike. And her expression? Carefully composed, just as if cooking and cleaning for them had been nothing but another job for her.

Just as if she hadn't had the same reaction he'd had when she'd visited him in his room.

His temper flared. "Kay, enough. And would you all give Elizabeth and me some privacy?"

All at once, Kaylene, Levi, Elizabeth, and Micah stopped what they were doing and stared at him in disbelief. Honestly, it was like he'd suddenly stood up and started singing and dancing at the top of his lungs.

"Why do you need privacy?" Levi asked.

"It's none of your business."

It used to be, he'd been able to stop Levi in his tracks by using just this tone of voice.

Now his sixteen-year-old brother merely looked bored. "I kind of think it is, seeing how I'm the one who invited her over here in the first place."

This seemed like an especially snarky comment, even for Levi. Lifting a brow, Randall glanced Micah's way.

But instead of backing him up, Micah merely shut his book and stood up. "Elizabeth, is this what you want? If not, I'll stay here with you."

To have one brother go against him was one thing. But now he had two of them? That was too much. "Hey, now—"

Micah glared at him. "Enough, *bruder.*" Softening his tone, he walked toward Elizabeth. "I do agree that it's time you stopped cleaning. I promise, this kitchen has never been so spotless, not even when Claire was at her most industrious. But if you'd rather go to your room, I'd understand."

He wouldn't! With effort, Randall kept his mouth shut. But he had now moved on from being irritated to very confused. His brothers were treating Elizabeth as if she were the person injured.

Actually, as if he had hurt her feelings!

"I'll be happy to chat with Randall for a few minutes before I head to bed," she said as she carefully folded the dishcloth and walked into the keeping room. Then, at last, she looked his way. "As a matter of fact, I think Randall and I have much to discuss."

"I'll be in the workshop if you need me," Micah said. "Kaylene, you can come with me or go with Levi to the basement or to your room."

"Couldn't I stay here if I stayed real quiet?"

"*Nee*," Randall said. "Go on with you, Kay."

With the speed of snails, his siblings at last eased out of the room, leaving him lying on the couch and Elizabeth perched on the chair across from him.

When they were at last alone, she raised a brow. "Well? What was it you wanted to talk about?"

Whether it was the shock of the news, the sight of Micah looking after her, almost trying to save her from him, or the frustration that had been building up from injuring himself doing something he'd been doing for years without a single mishap, he didn't know.

But he'd reached his boiling point.

"Elizabeth, no more skating around the issue," he blurted, all the tension and frustration and loneliness in his heart flying up to the forefront. "What in the world is going on with us?"

He felt no small measure of satisfaction when he noticed that now she looked just as flustered as he felt.

He couldn't have been happier about that.

Elizabeth's mouth went dry as Randall's words sank in. She didn't know whether to be disappointed, intrigued, or simply really, really irritated.

"Randall, you have the worst timing on the planet. This is neither the time nor the place to talk about our relationship."

"Why isn't it? I don't have any place else to go. Do you?"

"I can think of a lot of other things I'd rather be doing instead of rehashing our relationship."

Randall tilted his head. "Did we ever discuss our relationship in the first place?"

She felt a little stumped. Not until just that moment had she ever stopped to consider that maybe they never really had discussed their feelings or their future. "Do you mean while we were dating or when we broke up?" she asked, mainly to stall for time.

"I mean either." He shifted a bit. It was obvious that he was uncomfortable. Almost as uncomfortable with his sitting position as he was with the conversation. "Elizabeth, I know we courted for years. And that there were many unspoken expectations on both of our ends. But I can't really think of a time that I asked you how you felt about me."

"You didn't need to. You had to know I liked you. You were the one who never felt like sharing your feelings."

"Elizabeth, I've always thought you were pretty. And I liked your temperament. You were easy to get along with."

"We never fought. You were always in a good mood." She thought about it a little more. "And you never made me think too much. I started seeing you just as my *mamm* fell in love and moved away."

"I knew that happened and assumed it was difficult for you." He wrinkled his brow. "But did I ever actually ask you about how you felt about that?"

"I was glad you didn't. I didn't want to talk to you about how sad I was that Mamm found another person and was perfectly okay with leaving me."

Shocked at herself, she pressed her palm to her mouth. "Randall, I can't believe I just said that."

"I can't believe we never talked about it in the first place." He exhaled. "Elizabeth, no wonder we broke up so easily. We broke apart because we had so little keeping us together."

"That's not true. We had a lot. We were friends."

"And we liked the same people. Being with you was easy. Comfortable. I never had to try too hard."

"I see." She couldn't help feeling a bit hurt by his words. It sounded as if he'd purposely courted her because he didn't have to try hard to please her. She didn't especially like how that sounded . . . or how it made her feel.

He rubbed a hand over his cheek. "Look, I know I am making a mess of this. I know I am making things between us sound bad."

"That is true."

"What I'm trying to tell you is that I'm different now. Elizabeth, it's only been since we broke up that I've been trying harder. Something about taking the responsibility for my family helped me learn to really listen to people. To ask the right questions. To not take them for granted. And it's only been since you've been coming here that I feel like we've gotten close. And now you're leaving."

She hated how he was making it sound as if she was leaving him on purpose. "I need to leave, Randall."

"Why? Why tomorrow?" Looking at her curiously, he added, "Were you only here because it was a job?"

"Randall, you're making everything so convoluted," she said impatiently. "I wouldn't have come over here in the first place if you and Levi hadn't asked me to work here. I wouldn't have stayed here out of mere friendship. It would have been a little too awkward, don't you think?"

"Is that all I am to you? A job?"

"You know that's not true. But you're being terribly judgmental and naïve if you think I'm going to forget all about my financial needs. I don't have a group of brothers and sisters who would drop everything at a moment's notice to help. I don't live on a prosperous farm or have lots of money invested wisely. Today when Junior handed me that four hundred dollars? It was the first time I've ever had that much money in my hand. It's certainly the first time in a year that I'm going to actually be able to put something aside."

He looked away. "I knew things were tough for you, but I didn't realize you were so strapped."

"How could you?" she asked, knowing that her voice sounded harsh. "After you told me that we couldn't see each other anymore, we never talked until I came here to work for your family."

"If I had known you needed something, I would have lent you the money."

"And you think I would have taken it? Oh, Randall. Do you really even know me?"

"I thought I did. I think I do now. I am learning more about you every day. And guess what?"

"What?"

"Elizabeth, I'm glad we are still learning more about each other! It's makes our . . . relationship . . . feel brand-new."

She'd never thought about it quite like that. "I like it, too."

"So, does that mean you still like me?"

She stared, struggling with how much she was ready to reveal. Then she noticed how direct his gaze was, how honest. He looked vulnerable and uneasy. He looked exactly the same way she was feeling.

And while she wished that he was making the first move, she also realized that he was trying to protect himself. Here he was, immobile from a broken leg. Unable to reach for her. Unable to do anything but sit and wait for her response.

For the moment—maybe for the first time in their relationship—she was in control. Not him.

Slowly, she nodded. "I do still like you, Randall Beiler. Do you like me?"

"Elizabeth, I think I'm in love with you." While she gaped at him, he waved an impatient hand. "So where does that leave us?"

"I suppose you are going to have to figure out if you want to court me properly."

"And how do you think I should do that?"

She waved a hand. "Oh, no. I'm not going to tell you how to court me. You are a smart man, you can figure that out for yourself."

He groaned, but it was obvious it was all for show. "You drive a hard bargain, Elizabeth."

"I guess you'll just have to decide if I'm worth the trouble."

"You've always been worth it. I was the one who wasn't doing enough for you." Squirming a bit, he murmured, "But you've got me at a disadvantage, you know. I'm stuck in this house for at least a week. And even after that I won't be able to get around easily for a while."

"How is that a disadvantage?"

He practically rolled his eyes. "Elizabeth, how am I supposed to court you properly while I'm stuck in a cast? I may not be much for romance, but even I know that ain't how to treat a girl properly."

She didn't even try to hide her smile. "I don't know. But I feel sure and for certain that you'll be able to think of something."

He held out a hand. "Help me get back to my room?"

Clasping his hand, she nodded. "Of course."

When they got him to a standing position and were slowly making their way to his bedroom, he looked down at her. "Any chance I'll get a kiss good night?"

"Nope."

"Not even on the cheek?"

"Not even there," she said. "You may kiss my cheek when you are courting."

In reply, he leaned closer and placed his lips on her brow. "*Danke*, Beth. *Danke* for waiting for me. You won't regret it, I promise."

She had a feeling she already did not.

chapter twenty-five

Her house was so packed full of people, Judith was sure all of their neighbors assumed they were having a grand celebration. The reality couldn't be further from the truth.

Inside, there was enough tension in the room to cut with a knife. Hardly anyone was talking; most of the people were simply staring out the window.

As they had been for the last hour.

Never had the time gone so slowly. They were all awaiting the arrival of Kendra's sisters and their husbands.

Leaning close to her on the hard wooden bench against the wall of the entryway, Ben whispered, "Are you as surprised as I am that everyone came over?"

"*Jah*. I thought maybe Mamm or Daed would want to come over. Never everyone."

"This is a blessing, it is."

"To be sure." When Judith had told her parents Bernie's news, she'd known she'd find support from them. They'd always supported her in any way they could her whole life. But she hadn't expected them to immediately send Anson out on a mission to inform the rest of the family that they would all be needed at Judith and Ben's *haus* in two days' time.

When Judith had learned of the plot, she'd attempted to tell her *mamm* that having her whole family in her keeping room when Kendra's relatives arrived wasn't a good idea. A bunch of Grabers together was an invitation to hear everyone's opinions, whether they had been asked to share or not.

All Judith could think was that her gregarious family would scare off the sisters, not to mention upset baby James. But her mother had waved aside her misgivings in short order.

"Judith, I don't fault Kendra's sisters for wanting to see what kind of place baby James has found himself in. I'm sure they're curious. But if they are coming over to inspect the baby's life with you, then they need to see that James is not being adopted just by you and Ben. He's going to be adopted and loved by the whole family."

"You don't think we might be a bit, ah, overwhelming?"

Her mother had looked completely confused by the question. "And why would anyone think that?"

And just like that, she'd given in. Two days ago, Judith had been too overwhelmed to argue much. Especially when in the next breath her mother had begun to plan what they would be serving to the guests.

Any and all comments from Judith about how maybe they didn't need to serve a complete Amish dinner were ignored.

Now, as she looked around at Joshua, Gretta, and their two boys; Caleb and Rebecca; her parents; Anson; Toby; and little Maggie; and even Tim and Clara and their babies, Judith realized she'd never felt more blessed.

She'd also never felt more like it had been the right decision. James was currently chewing on an icy washcloth and playing with the edge of her mother's gray dress. He was dressed in tiny blue slacks and a little pale blue shirt. In his lap was a stuffed horse, which was his new favorite toy.

He looked Amish. He looked adorable.

As if he sensed her attention, he suddenly turned his head,

located her, then smiled a gummy, wet grin. "Ma . . . ma . . . ma . . . ma."

Though it was obvious he wasn't actually calling her "Ma," she knew she was the only mom he'd ever known.

She smiled back and felt the lump in her throat turn a little bit bigger. What was she going to do if Kendra's relatives decided that she and Ben weren't good enough for James?

"Don't think about that," Ben cautioned. "You need to stay positive."

She turned to him in surprise. "How did you know what I was thinking?"

"You're thinking and worrying so much, I can practically read your mind. But, I promise, don't do this to yourself. You need to hope for the best. And, dear wife, you need to remember what you always tell me."

"That the Lord will provide?"

"*Jah.*" His lips curved upward, but it vanished almost as quickly as he stared out the window. "Here we go."

She stood up, half expecting Anson or her mother, or any number of people to start announcing the obvious. Or offering suggestions to Judith.

Or doing any number of things that they usually did.

But everyone stayed seated and silent, almost as if they were afraid to do anything wrong. They were truly giving the phrase "being on their best behavior" a whole new meaning.

Ironically, their stiff postures eased her mood. "Come on, everyone, perk up," she said. "This isn't a funeral. All we're doing is getting to know James's aunts."

Gretta, looking as serene and dignified as ever, was the one person who broke the silence. "You're right, Judith. I don't know why we are all being so nervous."

To Judith's relief, Clara walked to her and linked her arm

in hers. "We are going to get through this with flying colors," she said. "If you need something, just look at one of us. We'll figure out how to get it for you." She smiled sweetly, now obviously not caring that she bore scars from a long-ago fire. "Or we'll be by your side in an instant."

"I appreciate that."

The knock on the door prevented anything else. And then, with a new set to his shoulders, Ben opened the door and said, *"Wilcom!"*

"Hi, Ben," Bernie said as she stepped inside. When she looked around the room and saw how many of their relatives were there, her eyes widened. "I see we're going to get to meet a lot of people this evening."

Judith stepped next to Ben. "Please come in, everyone. I am Judith Knox, and this is my husband, Ben."

In came Bernie and two African-American couples. They looked to be just a little bit older than Judith. After a pause, the lady closest to Judith held out a hand. "Hi, my name is Katherine Jensen, and this is my husband, Brendan. And this is my sister Emma and her husband, Patrick."

"Ben Knox," Ben said and shook everyone's hand, then closed the door behind the newcomers.

Katherine and Emma did the same thing Bernie had done; they looked a little taken aback by the crowd that greeted them. But then their gazes settled on baby James, who was staring right back at them with a wide-eyed, curious look.

"Is this him?" Katherine asked, her voice hoarse.

When Judith simply nodded, her mother saved the day. She popped James on her hip as she joined them. *"Jah,* this is your sweet nephew, James. And I am Irene Graber. I'm Judith's mother."

Katherine and Emma gazed at James in wonder. "He's

beautiful," Emma said. With a sad shake of her head, she added, "I can't believe I didn't want to see him. I can't believe I kept putting off my visit to Kendra, too. I was such a fool."

"Not a fool," her mother said. "We all think we have all the time in the world to make poor decisions, *jah*? Because we imagine that we'll always have all the time in the world to make things right."

Emma swallowed. "You are exactly right, Irene. I've made some terrible choices, and I'm having to live with those consequences now."

As she sighed, she looked weary. "The sad thing is that it's no less than I deserve. I had been so tired of Kendra making so many mistakes." She shook her head. "So many bad decisions."

"The drugs," Katherine said.

"And the men."

"Stealing."

Emma frowned. "For years, it seemed like we weren't supposed to do anything but bail her out, time and again."

"It was hard. Really hard," Katherine interjected.

"It got so I was so tired of her disappointing me that I wanted nothing to do with her."

"We could only take so much, you know?"

Reaching for her husband's hand, Emma continued. "Even when she was in jail, I told myself that it was going to hurt too much to make amends. Now it's too late."

Her husband wrapped an arm around her. "We've already gone through this, Emma. No good is going to come of you constantly castigating yourself."

She shook her head, then looked around at the others and grimaced. "I'm sorry. I didn't mean to come here and lay all my troubles at your feet."

"Our *haus* is yours," Ben said as he led them into the keeping room. "Please, will you sit down? And then, maybe you'd like to hold James?"

Katherine gazed at her husband. "We'd like nothing better," she said.

After a few more introductions, Gretta and Rebecca went to go get the trays they'd already prepared with cookies and coffee cups. Then the two couples sat, Bernie nearby, but unusually silent.

Just as her mother was about to place James in Katherine's arms, James frowned and squirmed. "Ma-ma-ma-ma,"

Emma frowned. "Is he saying what I think he is?"

James answered that one, looking at Judith and smiling brightly. He squealed, then held out his chubby arms to her.

Judith wasn't sure what to do. Did she dare take James and risk hurting his aunts' feelings? Or should she err on the side of ignoring his pleas? But then, if she did that, it would make it seem like she was a poor mother.

In the end, her heart led the way. She reached out, clasped James to her chest, and smiled as he cuddled close.

As she smelled his clean skin and felt his comfortable weight in her arms, she pressed her lips to his soft, curly head. Oh, she was going to miss James so much!

Belatedly she noticed that their visitors were staring at her and James in surprise.

"He loves you, doesn't he?" Katherine said in wonder.

"I hope so. I love him."

As an awkward silence settled in, Bernie saved the day. "Remember, everyone, nothing is going to be settled today. All this is, is a chance for some of James's relatives to meet him, and to meet the folks who've been his foster parents."

Emma and Katherine nodded, but Judith could tell they

were still awkwardly processing everything that they'd been observing.

But then the girls came in and drinks and cookies were served. Slowly everyone began talking. Joshua and his father told them about the Graber Country Store. Katherine's husband revealed that he was a doctor. Emma and Patrick talked about their own children.

At last, James settled down enough to let his aunts hold him. When Judith saw him in their arms, she felt a sense of loss but not the extreme dismay she had been expecting.

When he fell sound asleep, Katherine and Emma went with Judith to James's room. When they saw his cozy crib, the quilt-covered rocking chair, and the assortment of toys in a basket, they smiled.

When it was almost time to go, Emma said, "You know it's funny. I was really nervous about meeting all of you. I never met any Amish before. I thought you would be really backward. Or at least really different."

Bernie raised her brows. "The Grabers are good people, aren't they?"

"They are." Chuckling, Brendan said, "Next time we meet I'm going to ask for a buggy ride."

After glancing at their mom, Anson popped up on his feet. "We have something for you in the back of one of the buggies. Would you like to meet our new horse, Pam?"

"Its name is Pam?"

Anson shrugged. "She can't help her name, but she's making the best of it, I think."

Brendan nudged his wife. "Are you listening, dear? Anson is right."

When Brendan and Patrick went to go see the horse, Tim, Clara, and Judith's *daed* went out, too.

Rebecca and Gretta took the youngest kids into the kitchen, leaving Katherine, Emma, Bernie, Judith, and Ben in the room.

Bernie looked at the group assembled around her. "Perhaps we should talk a bit about what is going to happen next. Katherine and Emma, you asked for this meeting. You told me you wished to see where James has been in order to make the best decision about who should raise him."

She slipped on her glasses before turning to Judith and Ben. "As we said earlier, you did meet with Kendra and she had started to fill out the paperwork naming you two as James's parents before she passed away."

Judith clasped her hands on her lap. "I am glad we met. From the moment we met James, he's had my heart. But he's a *wonderful-gut* boy. I can understand wanting to be a part of his life, too."

Katherine leaned back. "You know, I've been living with regrets, regrets for my relationship with my sister, and for being too stubborn and prideful. Emma might feel differently, but after being here, I realize that James already has a family who loves him. He's happy here. He has a mom, and it's you. I can't be the person to take him away from that. He's already lost one mother, even though he doesn't know it yet."

Bernie leaned forward. "So you are saying that you would like for James to continue living here?"

Katherine nodded. "Yes. Permanently. But if you don't mind too much, I'd like him to know us, too."

"I'd like that, too," Judith murmured. "I want him to know you all."

Bernie opened up her notebook and wrote down some notes. "Emma, do you have any questions?"

She shook her head slowly. "Yesterday I realized that I already have my hands full with my own children. I was willing to take in James, but right now I'm thinking the same thing that my sister is. But it would be a further tragedy if I pulled him from here. I want to know him. I want to get to know all of you. But I don't want to raise him if he's happiest here."

Eyes twinkling, Bernie turned to Judith and Ben. "Now it's your turn. Mr. and Mrs. Graber, would you like to begin the formal process to make James your son?"

Judith could hardly swallow for the lump in her throat. Only when Ben clasped his hand over hers was she able to reply. "Yes, we would."

"And would you be willing to let James get to know his aunts, perhaps even spend time with them when he is older?"

"We would," Ben said. "Family is wonderful. I want him to know his real mother's family. I want him to know that many, many people love him."

Bernie clapped her hands together. "I couldn't be happier with how today's visit turned out. Ben and Judith, congratulations, it looks like you now have a son."

Judith felt like her heart would burst. "We are so blessed," Judith said, trying to hold back tears. "I am the most blessed woman in the whole world right now. And the happiest."

As she hugged her precious husband, she realized that she meant every single word. They were blessed beyond measure . . . and their hearts were so full of joy.

chapter twenty-six

"Lizzie, a buggy's coming up the drive," her grandmother announced from her rocking chair on the front porch.

Elizabeth groaned. Of course they had company. Folks always stopped by at the worst times—when she was a sweaty mess and covered with dirt, thanks to the last hour she'd spent weeding in the garden. Just one day she'd love to greet a visitor when she looked her best.

"Mommi, who is it? Can you tell?"

"Oh, *jah*, I can tell. It's Randall Beiler."

"Are you sure about that?"

"Mighty sure. There's only one horse in the area that is dapple gray. And there's only one man who holds the reins like he does."

She winced as she realized that her dress was sticking to her back. No doubt, she smelled, too. " Mommi, see if you can stall him a moment, wouldja? I've got to go get cleaned up."

"Don't think you'll have time for that, Lizzie. Randall is already getting out of his buggy. Oh, he's pulling something out of it. Flowers!"

Flowers? Oh, this news was getting worse and worse. Obviously, Randall was taking her up on her offer and was now determined to court her properly.

And that would have been wonderful—if she'd had any idea that he had been coming over.

"Try to stall him, Mommi!" The garden—such that it was—was a mere three yards from her back door. Eyeing it, she wondered if it would be possible to dart inside and change her dress. Looking at her dirty hands, she realized that she should wash up at the very least.

"I'll try, dear, but I don't think it's going to do much good."

"Why is that?"

"Because I'm already here," Randall said as he limped around the corner, one hand holding his bouquet of roses. His other hand had a sure grip on a wooden crutch.

"Look at you," she said. "You're getting around pretty good."

"I'm trying." Looking a bit embarrassed, he added, "You should have seen me the first couple of times I tried to get around. I just about landed on the floor. But now I'm getting the hang of it."

"I'll say. You are even showing up at houses unexpectedly."

"You don't need to sound quite so excited about my visit," he said sarcastically.

Looking into his eyes, she said, "Look at me, Randall. I'm in an old dress and covered with dirt." She waved a hand in the air. "And you? You're all dressed up. And you're holding roses."

He smiled, like he was glad she'd finally noticed the dozen pink roses nestled in a batch of baby's breath in his arms. "I think you look fine."

"Would you like to come inside? I'll pour you something to drink while I get cleaned up."

He shook his head. "Do you mind if I stay outside? It's a pretty June day. Too nice to be inside."

"How about I'll meet you on the porch in five minutes?" Elizabeth asked as she took the bouquet from him. Unable to help herself, she inhaled the scent. "The flowers are lovely, Randall. Really beautiful."

"I'm glad they please you."

She blinked, realizing that he was being completely honest. He'd gone to a lot of trouble to make sure she liked the roses. "They do. I'll be right back."

"Take your time. I'll wait."

After sending him a weak smile, she opened the door and darted inside. Everything about him was making her feel like she was on her first date with him.

Five minutes. She had five minutes to look fresh and pretty. Darting around the corner, she practically ran into her grandmother.

She held up her hands like she was worried Elizabeth was about to run her down. "Lizzie, watch yourself!"

"Mommi, would you please put these in water? I've got to go get presentable."

"*Jah*, dear." Wrinkling her nose, she murmured. "I do think it would be best if you freshened up a bit. How about I take out some cookies and lemonade to the porch? That is where Randall is, *jah*?"

"That would be so great," she called out over her shoulder as she practically scampered down the hall. "*Danke*, Mommi."

By the time she got to her room, she had her dress halfway unpinned. In record time she put on her favorite raspberry-colored dress and then was in the bathroom carefully washing every last bit of dirt from her hands and wiping down the back of her neck and forehead.

Hoping she at least smelled better, she raced to the front door, just as her grandmother was walking through it.

Eyeing her, Mommi closed the door with a snap. "Stop for

a moment, dear, and catch your breath. You look like you are frightened that you're going to be late for class—not about to be greeting a suitor."

The old-fashioned advice made Elizabeth smile, but she knew there was truth to her grandmother's words. Breathing deeply, she inhaled and exhaled. Then did it again.

"That's much better. Now, off you go."

Hoping her face wasn't as red as her dress, Elizabeth opened the door and quietly walked out.

"You didn't make it," Randall said as she took the rocking chair next to him.

"What?"

"Fact is, I've been counting, and it's taken you almost ten minutes to come back down to me."

"Sorry."

"Don't be. It was worth the wait. You look much more like yourself now." The corners of his lips turned up, as if he had a secret joke. "Though we both know I've seen you the other way a time or two."

"Tell me why you're here, with roses no less."

"I think we both know why. I wanted to see you. I wanted to come calling and show you that I still care about you. I was serious about my intentions, Elizabeth."

She smiled at him, wanting to say so much but still afraid to say too much. Still guarding her heart.

Needing to say something, though, she blurted, "So, um, how are things at your *haus*?"

After looking at her for a long moment, he shrugged. "We're a mess. But I have learned to grill pork chops, so things have improved a bit."

She smiled. "How are those baked potatoes coming along?"

"About the same." He chuckled. "Actually, my poor skills

228 • Shelley Shepard Gray

have shamed Levi and Micah into trying their hand at other side dishes. Neil has now mastered rice. And Levi's mashed potatoes are almost edible now. And Micah has proved his fancy education is paying off. He followed the directions on a box of Jell-O the other day. It set up like a charm."

"Impressive." Her lips twitched as she tried to hold off a giggle. "Before you know it, you won't remember why you needed me."

"Never," he replied, his voice turning serious. "Now I realize why everything was so special when you were there. And though you are a wonderful cook, the food had nothing to do with it."

"Oh?"

"It was you, Elizabeth. You lit up our house with your chatter and your smiles. The halls shone, not because you are so handy with a mop, but because you brought us all happiness. Now that you're gone, our house feels empty."

His honesty made her want to be honest, too. "It hasn't been the same here, either. My grandmother and I have never been so unimpressed with clean countertops and organized closets."

"When I get better, I am hoping that maybe we can go on some walks this summer. Maybe even go to the flea market a time or two."

"Randall—"

"Or if that doesn't suit you, maybe I can take you out to eat," he continued in a rush. "That would be nice, don't you think? Supper out so you don't have to cook?"

"That would be mighty nice, but—"

He cut her off, looking vaguely panicked. "Or, if you'd rather, I'll keep coming over. And I'll bring more flowers, too."

"I don't need more flowers."

"Sure you do. I need to make sure you feel special, Beth."

She couldn't help herself. She started laughing. Then she started laughing so hard she couldn't stop.

But instead of laughing with her, Randall started looking a little green. "Are you laughing at me? Have I completely messed everything up?"

She stood up. "Not at all. What I've been trying to tell you is that I'm already yours. You don't need to do all that."

"What are you saying?"

"Exactly what you think I am," she replied, unable to hide another thing from him. She was sure she was positively beaming. "I still love you, Randall Beiler. And you already do make me feel special."

Bracing a hand on the heavy table next to him, he got to his feet. "Does this mean you're still my girl?"

She nodded.

"And that one day, you'll marry me?"

"Are you asking?"

"Well, I'm trying." Reaching out, Randall linked his fingers with hers, glancing at her face, trying to gauge if she was amused. If he was messing up this most important moment.

Maybe she had hoped for sweeter words. More romance. Maybe he should have brought along flowers *and* chocolate?

Those worries passed as he saw her expression. Her eyes were bright with joy, her lips were slightly parted.

"Randall, are ya ready?" she gently prodded.

He swallowed. Lifted one of her hands and brought it to his lips. Kissed her knuckles.

Then, at long last he was ready. "Elizabeth, you now know how much I love you. It's also obvious that I need you something awful. You make me a better man. I don't ever want to be without you again."

Quickly, he peeked at her expression. Tears glistened in her eyes now. Happy tears.

He kissed her knuckles again.

"Beth, I think I could stand here for hours and tell you all the things I like about you. I could tell you that I've always thought your brown eyes were pretty. That I've always thought you were lovely. That I've never forgotten the first time I heard you laugh. But I'm too anxious for that."

She squeezed his hands. "Just ask me, Randall."

"All right. Elizabeth Nolt, would you marry me? Marry me so I won't be without you any longer? Marry me so I can hear your laughter in our house? Marry me so you'll always be mine?"

Those were the words she'd always hoped he'd say. Words she'd always hoped to hear.

And so, because of that, there was only one answer.

"Of course, Randall Beiler. Of course I will marry you."

He breathed a sigh of relief—just before he wrapped his arms around her and kissed her.

And when she lifted her arms and wrapped them around his neck, Elizabeth at last discovered what it felt like to be completely wanted and needed and loved.

And her heart filled with joy. So much joy.

Surely enough to last a whole lifetime.

epilogue

Fall had come again to Sugarcreek. The sky was a lovely robin's-egg blue, the trees dotting the countryside were glistening in vibrant shades of gold and red, and most of the shops and restaurants in town had mums decorating their doorsteps.

The Grabers' store had two wheelbarrows full of pumpkins on the front porch and the Sugarcreek Inn was offering a special on their pumpkin pie.

As Randall Beiler strolled down the sidewalk by his wife's side, he took note of everything. Liked how some things never changed.

As his gaze darted to the crowd of people in front of him, all of whom happened to be related to him by birth or by marriage, he also reflected how happy he was that some things changed a lot.

When they stopped at the front door of the Sugarcreek Inn, Junior faced them all. Obviously it didn't matter how old they were—he was determined to always, always be in charge.

Junior's eyes darted around the lot of them. "Do we have everyone?"

"Yep," Levi said.

"Sure?"

Micah sighed. "*Bruder, jah*. We are all here. All thirteen of us."

"I thought there were only twelve?"

"Miriam's holding your namesake, *Albert*. We've got eight Beilers, four spouses, and one baby boy. Thirteen."

"Impressive counting," Beverly murmured.

"I am the smartest one, you know," Micah quipped.

Just as he had when he was a little boy, Junior scowled at the use of his real name. "I'm just trying to keep track of everyone. It's not often that we go out to eat, you know."

Before Randall could comment about that, Miriam Beiler curved the hand that wasn't cradling Albert around her husband's arm. "Luckily for everyone involved, I know this restaurant well," she said quickly. "*Danke* for coming out today. I know this means a lot to everyone."

Claire nodded. "It's a special day, to be sure."

At last, Junior opened the door and the rest of them filed by, each entering the restaurant almost silently. At the end of the group was little Kaylene, who at almost ten years of age wasn't quite so little anymore.

But she still grasped her big brother's hand when he held it out, smiling sweetly at him when they entered the dining room.

Pippa Reyes met them, a shiny new diamond engagement ring sparkling on her left hand. "Everything's ready," she said with a smile. "We set up all the tables just the way you wanted them, too," she said.

Randall squeezed Elizabeth's hand as they followed Junior and Kaylene to the long line of tables and fifteen chairs.

After everyone sat down, taking care to leave the two chairs empty at either end, Randall stood up. Last night, he'd told Junior that he'd like to do the talking, both of them knowing that though Junior was still the head of their family, he would be too choked up to do the occasion justice.

After clearing his throat, he said, "Over the years, our family has been through some hardships. We've also had our share of celebrations. I think we Beilers have always had our moments when we've asked the Lord why things happened the way they did. It wasn't easy losing Mamm and Daed. It hasn't been easy raising ourselves, either. But as I look around at all of us, including Junior's Junior, I am more certain than ever that we all turned out okay." He paused, smiled at his older sisters. "Maybe better than okay."

He cleared his throat. "Anyway, now that things are settled."

"More or less," Levi quipped.

"More or less. Junior and I decided that we should commemorate it. Such that it is."

Taking a deep breath, he pushed through the lump in his throat and finished things up. "Today marks what would have been our parents' thirtieth anniversary. I thought it was fitting that we remember this day, the day our parents began our family." He looked at the empty chairs, remembering earlier years, years when both his parents filled the spaces . . . and those sad years when only their father did.

He remembered Levi having nightmares and Kaylene feeling guilty for being born. He remembered standing by gravesides and joining the rest of the family in Junior's living room while they waited for Miriam to give birth.

But most of all he remembered always knowing, that no matter what, he was never alone. The bond he had with his siblings was the strongest bond he had. Irrefutable. Solid. Special.

Everything.

He reached out and picked up his glass of water. "So, um, with that in mind, I'd like to raise a toast to Mamm and

Daed, and to make a promise that wherever I am, no matter what, I will always be with you all on October first. And I'm asking you all to make that promise, too."

After a brief burst of silence, the lot of them raised their glasses and nodded.

And with that, he sat down. Hopeful for their future. Thankful for their past. Joyful in his heart.

And realizing that sometimes . . . sometimes, not a single word ever needed to be said.

Everything was understood.

About the author

About the book

Read on

Insights,
Interviews
& More . . .

Meet
Shelley Shepard Gray

The New Studio

PEOPLE OFTEN ASK how I started writing. Some believe I've been a writer all my life; others ask if I've always felt I had a story I needed to tell. I'm afraid my reasons couldn't be more different. See, I started writing one day because I didn't have anything to read.

I've always loved to read. I was the girl in the back of the classroom with her nose in a book, the mom who kept a couple of novels in her car to read during soccer practice, the person who made weekly visits to the bookstore and the library.

Back when I taught elementary school, I used to read during my lunch breaks.

One day, when I realized I'd forgotten to bring something to read, I turned on my computer and took a leap of faith. Feeling a little like I was doing something wrong, I typed those first words: *Chapter One.*

I didn't start writing with the intent of publishing a book. Actually, I just wrote for myself.

For the most part, I still write for myself, which is why, I think, I'm able to write so much. I write books that I'd like to read. Books that I would have liked to have in my old teacher tote bag. I'm always relieved and surprised and so happy when other people want to read my books, too!

Another question I'm often asked is why I choose to write inspirational fiction. Maybe at first glance, it does seem surprising. I'm not the type of person who usually talks about my faith in the line at the grocery store or when I'm out to lunch with friends. For me, my faith has always felt like more of a private thing. I feel that I'm still on my faith journey—still learning and studying God's word.

And that, I think, is why writing inspirational fiction is such a good fit for me. I enjoy writing about characters who happen to be in the middle of their faith journeys, too. They're not perfect, and they don't always make the right decisions. Sometimes they make mistakes, and sometimes they do something they're proud of. They're characters who are a lot like me.

Only God knows what else He has in store for me. He's given me the will ▶

Meet Shelley Shepard Gray *(continued)*

and the ability to write stories to glorify Him. He's put many people in my life who are supportive and caring. I feel blessed and thankful . . . and excited to see what will happen next! ∼

What's on Shelley Shepard Gray's Bookshelf?

IT'S NOT A BIG SECRET. I read a lot. Usually two to three books a week. I also like to read all kinds of books— and I also reread favorites over and over.

Here are ten books that currently have my attention. Next week? The list will probably look very different!

Running Blind by Lee Child.

My husband and I really enjoy Lee Child's books. I'm currently reading them out loud to my husband when we go on road trips.

The Bedwyn Saga books by Mary Balogh.

Oh, Mary Balogh. She's so, so talented. I've already read this whole series but I couldn't resist reading them again. Yes, all six of them.

Shattered by Dani Pettrey.

I have an awful habit of reading books when things are slow at my book signings. I picked this up at the Gospel Book Shop in Sugarcreek. So far, I'm loving it!

Death on Blackheath by Anne Perry.

Anne Perry is my very favorite author. I love her Victorian mysteries, especially the ones featuring Charlotte and Thomas Pitt. The folks at my neighborhood Barnes & Noble know to put each new ▶

5

What's on Shelley Shepard Gray's Bookshelf? *(continued)*

hardcover aside for me when Anne's books are released. I always buy them the day they come out, and I always take my time reading them.

Killing Jesus **by Bill O'Reilly.**
We've reading this in my small group at church. So far, we've had some great discussions.

Outlander **by Diana Gabaldon.**
Those of you who've read this know why it's on my bookshelf.

All of Robyn Carr's books.
I'm a fan of hers.

The Encyclopedia of Chicago **by James R. Grossman.**
I'm writing a couple of historical novels set during the 1893 Chicago World's Fair. This book has been invaluable to me.

The Measure of Katie Calloway **by Serena B. Miller.**
It's a great, award-winning historical novel set in a logging camp.

Murder in Thrall **by Anne Cleeland.**
This is a contemporary Scotland Yard mystery. ❧

Letter from the Author

Dear Reader,

Thank you for joining me for another visit to Sugarcreek! I hope you enjoyed getting to know Miriam and Elizabeth and Christina, the Beilers, Aden, Jana, Pippa, and, of course, James.

As with most of my books, the title was a guiding point for me. I spent a lot of time thinking about "joy" and how it relates to my faith, my family, romance, and hope. I even had some discussions with Mary, the cover designer, about what a joyful heroine should look like! I'm sure that was a bit challenging for her, because I'm pretty good at describing characters' personalities, but not nearly as good at describing what the characters look like in my head.

One night I was talking to my husband about "joy," discussing themes and things that brought joy in life when all of a sudden we looked at each other and smiled.

When our son, Arthur, was a baby, Tom and I were pretty young. We didn't live near any family, so most of the time we would do our best and hope it was good enough. I'm only sharing this because I think God gave us a little present right about the time Art was four months old. See, he had a double smile. When he was happy, he smiled. But when he was really happy? Really, absolutely delighted? His expression would be just a little bit ▶

7

brighter, his smile a little bit bigger. We used to live for those double-smile moments . . . that instant of pure joy.

I've felt joy at church, with my writing buddies, with my husband when we're just simply happy. In the kitchen when I have time to make cookies. When I'm sitting on the couch reading a good book next to my dachshunds. Lots of simple, everyday moments when I realize that I am probably wearing a double-smile of my own.

I hope you, too, find many moments in your life for double smiles and joy.

As always, thank you for reading my books. Thank you for sharing them with friends and family. And thank you, too, for giving me so much joy.

Shelley Shepard Gray
10663 Loveland, Madeira Rd. #167,
Loveland, OH 45140

Questions for Discussion

1. The guiding scripture verse for Joyful was from Psalm 97:11: *Light shines on the godly, and joy on those whose hearts are right.* While writing the novel, I thought a lot about the joy I feel in my relationship with the Lord. What does the verse make you think about?

2. I really felt that the following Amish Proverb fit the Beiler family: *A house is made from walls and beams . . . A home is made of love and dreams.* How have you made your house into a home?

3. The concept of "family" and the things that make a family was one of the themes I thought about when writing the novel. What do you think makes a family? How do the dynamics change over time?

4. Randall makes a lot of mistakes in his journey toward finding love with Elizabeth. Should Elizabeth have forgiven him so easily? How would you have reacted to his decisions?

5. What did you think about Elizabeth and her actions toward Randall? Does she grow as a character?

6. Which Beiler family member would you like to see fall in love next?

7. The journey toward parenthood for Judith and Ben was an especially difficult one. What do you think ▶

will happen with them in the future? Do you think James will be their only child, or do you think they'd be willing to go through so much again for another child?

8. One of my favorite scenes is when Judith gets some needed advice from her mother. What is the best piece of advice that you've received from your mother about motherhood? ∾

A Sneak Peek of Shelley Shepard Gray's Next Book, *Snowfall*

MARTIN HAD BECOME A MASTER at sipping a coffee and pretending that he wasn't nearly as worried as he actually was. But if there was ever a time when he found it rather difficult, it was this morning.

And that was because they were currently waiting for one Ruth Stutzman. He knew next to nothing about her. They belonged to different church districts. He couldn't remember ever meeting her in town, either.

Though that shouldn't have been a great surprise. He didn't ever notice women, even women whom his friends slyly mentioned were giving him special smiles or were going out of their way to chat with him. As far as he was concerned, his heart belonged to Grace and it always would.

After walking to the stove and warming up his cup, Martin realized that he didn't know much about Ruth Stutzman at all. Only that she was a friend of Lovina Keim's and that she'd agreed to take a leave of absence from her job at the retirement home to help him care for his children during Christmas break.

Everything about the situation grated on him. He didn't like the fact that Lovina Keim had called him last night after eight o'clock and informed him that she'd found him a new babysitter. ▶

11

When he'd asked how such a thing had come about, she'd relayed that she'd told Ruth all about him. And all about his motherless *kinner*. And how he couldn't cook and he was in dire need of a helping hand. Or several helping hands.

He'd been so appalled, he'd almost hung up.

But because he had no idea how to contact this Ruth, and he had no other option for the children other than packing them up and taking them to work at the Christmas tree farm, he'd instead conveyed his thanks.

But that didn't mean he liked being known as a helpless widower, or that he appreciated that folks at the Daybreak Retirement Home were talking about him.

It hurt a man's pride to be thought of as a charity case.

It almost physically hurt to realize that he was going to have to accept this Ruth Stutzman's help no matter what. He was that desperate. The trees weren't going to get chopped and transported by themselves. It was his job. Which was why he'd said yes to Ruth, though just imagining what Ruth was like made him cringe.

Already he was imagining an older woman with a bossy nature. After all, who else but a woman like that would be friends with Lovina Keim?

No doubt she would barely tolerate his brood, frown a lot, and speak her mind even when no one asked for her opinion.

If they were lucky.

And though he would never allow a woman into his home who would be mean to his *kinner*, he was enough of a realist to realize that taking care of six *kinner* like his was enough to make even the kindest and patient of women become a bit shrewish. Even his lovely Grace had lost her patience a time or two over the course of a day.

And because of that, Martin knew his children would be sad and miserable. And, perhaps, a touch resentful that while their many friends were out playing, baking cookies, and doing whatever else small children liked to do over Christmas breaks, they were having to spend their days in the company of a grumpy old woman named Ruth.

And after working all day at the Christmas tree farm, he was going to have to return each day, prepared to listen and cajole his children to try to deal with Ruth just a little bit longer.

He loved his children dearly. He'd loved his Grace, too, and had been delighted that she'd wanted such a big family. And for a time, their lives had seemed charmed.

And then not so charmed at all.

Yes, the Lord had shown him time and again that wishes and dreams didn't always count for much.

It had been a difficult lesson to learn but it had also been a valuable one.

"Daed, do you see her?" Thomas asked from the doorway leading into the dining room that they never used anymore.

"Not yet."

"Is she late?"

Thomas was a busy, buzzing child. As restless as a beaver on holiday and twice as inquisitive. "*Nee*, son. She ain't late yet."

"Then why are you staring out the window and frowning?"

"I'm simply looking out the window and thinking. There's a difference."

"Ah." Pulling over one of the dining room chairs, Thomas settled by his side and mimicked his pose. "What are you thinking about?"

"This and that."

"Are you thinking about Christmas?" His question had just the right amount of hope in it to make Martin's lips curve up.

"I'm thinking about Christmas trees."

Thomas sighed. "That's all you think about."

"That is not true. I think about lots of other things, too."

"But mainly you think about trees."

Not in any hurry to share just how much he worried about Thomas and his siblings, Martin lifted his chin. "Son, those trees occupy a good portion of my mind these days for a *gut* reason. They're important to our livelihood. We need to sell lots of trees this year."

"Oh? Do ya think, maybe, we could have a tree in our house?"

At least one of the children asked this every year. "Nope."

"Even if it was a small, ugly one?"

"Not even then." ▸

Thomas swung his feet. Shifted. Stood up and pressed his nose to the cold windowpane. After staring out the window thirty seconds, it was obvious he was bored. "Can I come with you today? I could help."

"Nope."

"Why not?"

"Because we're cutting and loading trees today, son."

"I could help."

"I'm afraid you can't. It's dangerous work. I don't want you to get hurt."

He straightened his narrow shoulders. "I'm pretty strong."

It took everything Martin had to keep a serious expression. "You are a mighty fine boy. And you are strong for being only eight. But I'm afraid you're not big enough to help. Not yet. One day you will, though."

"When? Next year?"

"I'm thinking when you're twelve."

Thomas's eyes widened, then settled into his scowl. "That's forever from now."

"You should enjoy being eight, then."

"I'm sick of staying home with old ladies."

Resting his hand on his boy's shoulders, Martin added, "I know it's hard, but someone needs to look after you all."

"It's boring. All Mrs. Keim wanted to do was sit in the kitchen and watch the clock."

Martin figured it would be best to say nothing about that. "Regardless, I have a feeling someday you'll be working so hard you'll be wishing for days like this."

"Days when I'm waiting for another grumpy babysitter? I don't think so."

"We don't know for sure if this one will be grumpy."

"Daed, she works with old people all day," Thomas said with the supreme confidence that only a child could have. "She's gonna be grumpy."

Since Martin felt his son had a point, he pressed his lips together and started simply hoping for a reprieve from the questions.

It was almost a relief to see the horse and buggy clip-clopping up the driveway. "We shall soon find out, won't we?" Turning, he saw that his Katrina had the rest of the *kinner* lined up against the window in the other room. They were standing in front of the window and looking out with various expressions of forbearance and dismay.

He stood up and carefully tucked his chair back to the kitchen table and motioned for Thomas to do the same. Then he stepped into the dining room and quietly spoke. "You all stay here while I go out and greet Ruth."

"Can you make sure she's nice, Daed?" Meg asked, her eyes filled with hope.

Reaching out, he pressed his hand on the top of his youngest child's *kapp*. "I will do my best," he promised.

While the children watched, Martin slipped on his coat, positioned his black stocking cap on his head, then walked out the door just as the buggy came to a stop in front of one of the hitching posts in front of the house, hoping all the while that this Ruth was going to be nicer than he expected her to be.

"Please, Lord," he quietly prayed. "Please, just give me a little bit of a break, wouldja? 'Cause I could surely use some help here. Make this woman not be too terrible. My *kinner* have already lost their mother. They don't need a sourpuss babysitter, too."

As the cold wind brushed against his cheeks, he lifted his eyes to the heavens and gave a fierce look. Then, as Ruth's horse pawed at the dry, hard ground restlessly, he hurried over to help. "Hello," he called out.

Just as Ruth Stutzman deftly hopped out of the buggy. Their eyes met. After the briefest of pauses, she smiled.

Martin blinked. And then, to his embarrassment, he blinked again, just as if he'd never seen a woman before.

Ruth Stutzman was young. And pretty, too. She had dark, wavy hair and pale, crystal-blue eyes. A smattering of freckles danced across her nose and the palest of pinks brightened her cheeks. She was of medium height and blessed with the kind of curves he'd always imagined women should have but always tried hard not to think about.

Maybe because she'd caught him so off guard. Or maybe because he was sadly out of practice when it came to conversing ▶

with pretty women, he blurted the first thing that came to mind. "You are nothing like I expected."

Raising a pair of finely arched eyebrows, her smile turned into a full-fledged grin. "Isn't that something? I was just thinking the same thing about you."

Martin was not sure if that was a compliment or not. And because he was so confused about his reaction, he turned away and grabbed hold of the horse. "It's too cold for your horse to be out here for long. I'll take him into the barn."

"I've got a blanket for him in the back of the buggy. Would you like me to cover him for you?"

"*Nee.*"

She stared at him, obviously waiting for him to finish his thought. To explain himself.

But he did neither. He simply stood still, holding the gelding's reins. He had never been a man of many words.

But suddenly, well, absolutely not a single one came to mind. Not a single, solitary one. ∽